FRIEND
OF THE
DEVIL

FRIEND
OF THE
DEVIL

STEPHEN LLOYD

G. P. PUTNAM'S SONS
NEW YORK

PUTNAM
— EST. 1838 —

G. P. Putnam's Sons
Publishers Since 1838
An imprint of Penguin Random House LLC
penguinrandomhouse.com

Library of Congress Cataloging-in-Publication Data
Names: Lloyd, Stephen (Television writer and producer), author.
Title: Friend of the devil / Stephen Lloyd.
Description: New York : G. P. Putnam's Sons, [2022] |
Identifiers: LCCN 2021055199 (print) | LCCN 2021055200 (ebook) |
ISBN 9780593331385 (hardcover) | ISBN 9780593331392 (ebook)
Subjects: LCGFT: Thrillers (Fiction) | Horror fiction. | Noir fiction. | Novels.
Classification: LCC PS3612.L694 F75 2022 (print) |
LCC PS3612.L694 (ebook) |
DDC 813/.6—dc23/eng/20211109
LC record available at https://lccn.loc.gov/2021055199
LC ebook record available at https://lccn.loc.gov/2021055200

Printed in the United States of America
1st Printing

BOOK DESIGN BY KRISTIN DEL ROSARIO

Title page art: Wrinkled paper © Arctic ice/Shutterstock.com

To my mother,
Arline Walsh Lloyd

FRIEND

OF THE

DEVIL

DANFORTH PUTNAM

A Wham-O Frisbee with a spinning yin-and-yang symbol sailed over the quad, disappeared for a moment in the sun, then wafted downward until a leaping Rottweiler dragged it to earth in its jaws. A gaggle of barefoot teenage boys with facial hair dyed unnatural colors and twisted into pitchforks or pincers tousled the Rottweiler's head. A dozen starved-looking kids from the cross-country team, punished by the unfairly warm October day, sprinted past in a glistening blur of Dolfin shorts. An Asian boy with an orange Mohawk wearing a sleeveless Black Flag T-shirt, camo pants, combat boots and a dog collar dabbed at fresh piercings with a Union Jack bandanna he moistened in rubbing alcohol. He scuttled between a pair of glossed and pretty teenage girls who shared grimaces and "Icks" with their glossed and pretty teenage boyfriends, the four of them tall, blond, tanned and sockless in Top-Siders, khakis and pastel Lacoste tennis shirts. A tall, pimply kid wearing a navy blazer and a Ronald Reagan button the size of a hubcap marched up to a small girl with a crew cut and dressed in a flannel shirt who was waving a pink triangle poster. He attempted to rip the poster, but she smacked his glasses off and called him a Nazi, and he skulked away, cursing.

It was a diverse group, Sam noted, in every way but one. They were all filthy rich. At least that's what Sam assumed. He didn't really know what the tuition at a school like this was, but it had to be astronomical. They had their own island, for Christ's sake, twenty square miles off the Massachusetts coast. On it were indoor and outdoor tennis courts, basketball courts, squash courts, Olympic-size pools, a soccer field, a football stadium, a hockey rink, horse stables (for the polo and equestrian teams), a television studio, three theaters and a science lab you could probably smash atoms in. Every building looked like it had been painted yesterday, and the surrounding lawns, hedge paths, rosebushes and topiaries were so meticulously groomed they made his marine buzz cut look shaggy.

Sam sparked his Zippo and lit a Kent. A squat, imperious woman leading a dozen small kids (too small to be in high school, he noted) scowled at him and sniffed at his cigarette.

He smiled at her with a lascivious wink and French-inhaled luxuriously until she huffed away, her small train in tow.

"What'd the cops say?" Sam asked the headmaster as they ambled across the quad.

Thomas Arundel was a large man with what Sam noticed was a great head of hair for a guy his age. It had gone gray, some of it white, but every follicle he'd ever had appeared to still be rooted. Tom's head, Sam thought, did not match his body. Above the neck, with his distinguished silver mane, wire-rimmed glasses and unblemished skin, he was the picture of an effete academic. Below the neck, with his rough, powerful bulk and hands the size of catchers' mitts, he looked like a dockworker or a former defensive tackle.

"They sent a patrolman. Not a detective. A kid in uniform barely old enough to shave," the headmaster said. "He did a full twenty minutes of investigating, which mostly involved striking up conversations with pretty female students. Since then, I've left five unreturned messages."

The yin-and-yang Frisbee bounced off the headmaster's chest and into one of his giant hands. Several players froze, staring at him and cringing.

"Gentlemen," the headmaster said. He closed his hand and snapped the Frisbee in half, as though it were made of tinfoil, the hard plastic cracking like gunfire. "Do be more careful." He neatly stacked the Frisbee halves and handed them to a chastened lad, who silently backed away.

Sam caught himself gaping and clamped his lips around the cigarette just before it tumbled out of his mouth. "Cops know how much the book's worth?"

Tom sighed. "Danforth Putnam is technically in West Cabot County. Last year, West Cabot County had three murders, two dozen rapes, nearly four hundred aggravated assaults and eighteen arsons. I called about a stolen book. Trust me, Mr. Gregory, they don't *care* what it's worth. As far as anyone on that side of the Atlantic is concerned, this is an island full of spoiled rich kids with spoiled-rich-kid problems, and a stolen book, even a valuable one, fits firmly in that category."

Sam more or less agreed with those on that side of the Atlantic. "A place like this, obviously you have your own security."

"And they're very well paid," said Tom irritably. "So far, they've turned up nothing."

"Well, wait till I get their reports before you fire any of them," said Sam. His eyes fell on the Asian kid with the orange Mohawk and piercings. "Halloween a few days early this year?"

The headmaster glanced at the Asian boy and sighed. "Today's youth, Mr. Gregory."

2

THE LIBRARY

S am found himself before the same woman who'd glow-ered at him for smoking on the quad. There were five feet to her, tops, carried mostly in the torso with her enormous bosom and bullfrog neck. She looked unnaturally white, with wet black eyes pushed deep into her pale, doughy face beneath eyebrows that seemed frozen in angry arches. She looked like a snowman that had been brought to life and was none too happy about it. When she saw Sam, her mouth twisted into a citrus pucker. "May I help you?" she asked in a voice that could freeze pipes.

"You're Ms. Lee, the head librarian?"

"I am," Ms. Lee said with a slow blink, fingering her necklace.

"My name's Sam Gregory," he said. "I'm an insurance investigator for SATCO Mutual."

She snorted. "I know what you are."

Sam tilted his head and gave her a smile. "You know, as a private investigator, I've gotten very good at reading people. So let's stop playing games. Obviously, you're into me. Is there a Mr. Ms. Lee?"

"I just think that, perhaps, we resorted to you rather quickly," Ms. Lee said. "We might have made some effort to find the book ourselves before summoning the likes of you to prowl about the school grounds."

The likes of me, Sam thought. Charming. He wasn't entirely sure of his ancestry. It was likely a mishmash of things, because he confused pretty much everyone who looked at him. Maybe she didn't like being confused. Maybe his tattoo read a little more roughneck than she liked. Or maybe he was there because of her screwup and she just didn't want that coming out. Time would tell.

"I'm awful sorry you find my presence here so distasteful, Ms. Lee, and I will do my best not to sully the school grounds with my prowling. In fact, I can wrap this up real quick if you want to withdraw your insurance claim. How's that sound?"

Ms. Lee fingered her necklace again and muttered a few words.

"Excuse me?" Sam asked.

"Please get on with your investigation, Mr. Gregory," she said.

He took out a notebook and pencil. "You recently reported the loss slash theft of an eleventh-century manuscript, is that right?"

"There was no loss slash, just theft, and would you mind refraining from that disgusting habit while on school grounds?"

Sam looked from her to his notebook. "Writing?"

"Smoking," Ms. Lee said. "Children live here."

Sam smiled. "Yeah, the ones I saw on the quad with you looked a little young for high school." He glanced around. "Ashtray?"

She took his cigarette between her thumb and forefinger, holding it at arm's length as if it were the tail of a dead rat, and stubbed it out in a teacup saucer. "I oversee all the children from the lower campus," she said. "That's for grades three to seven."

"You have *third*-graders at a boarding school?"

"There are women who marry men with children from previous marriages they don't want to be reminded of," Ms. Lee explained. "There are wealthy foreigners who want their children well away from the dangers of their homeland. And then there are the foundlings."

"Foundlings?"

"Orphans," said Ms. Lee, pronouncing the word slowly and loudly as though for someone new to English. "Danforth Putnam isn't merely an elite boarding school. It also runs the oldest continuously operating home for orphans in the United States. Since 1654, boys and girls as young as eight have been boarded and raised and taught here for free. Danforth Putnam is first and foremost a philanthropic institution."

Sam nodded. "Your cat is drinking your tea."

Ms. Lee turned to see a black cat, having noiselessly leapt onto her desk, now whiskers-deep in her Earl Grey. "Crowley, down!" she said, shoving the cat airborne.

Sam tapped his notebook with his pencil. "Report says the book was in a safe?"

Ms. Lee sniffed, grabbed a cane propped against the wall behind her and walked over to a large portrait of a Puritan with a broad, flat nose, a square jaw, shoulder-length brown hair and the smuggest smile Sam had ever seen. The smile seemed wildly out of place on a Puritan. He had assumed Puritans spent their whole lives scowling with disapproval. The frame was inscribed MASON ALDERHUT—FOUNDER.

Ms. Lee removed the portrait, revealing a wall safe, which she opened. "I'm not sure how they cracked it, but I plan to write a very strongly worded letter to the manufacturer."

Sam glanced at the safe, then returned to writing. "What you have there, Ms. Lee, is an Etson 5000 series. It has nylon wheels, false tumbler notches and a bunch of other neato stuff that means it can't be cracked without explosives. And since parts of it aren't strewn all over your carpet, whoever opened it had the combo, which ain't the manufacturer's fault. So, who knows the combo?"

"Well . . . just the headmaster and I," she said.

"You write it down someplace someone might have seen?" asked Sam.

"Why, yes, Mr. Gregory," said Ms. Lee, "that's exactly the kind of careless boob I am. Normally, I just leave the combination on a Post-it note stuck to the safe. That's, of course, when I bother to close it. Generally, I just leave it wide open with a hand-painted sign over it that reads RARE BOOKS INSIDE: PLEASE STEAL." She slammed the safe closed. "I didn't *give* anyone the combination, Mr. Gregory, mistakenly or otherwise, and neither did the headmaster."

Sam kept writing. "They take anything else?"

"Not that I've noticed," said Ms. Lee. She nodded at the window behind him. "That's how they got in."

"Tried the door first," Sam murmured as he made notes.

"Excuse me?" asked Ms. Lee.

Sam looked up as though noticing she was still there. "There are scuff marks around the spring latch in your office door from a screwdriver." Ms. Lee moved over to the door and bent to squint at the bent lock strike.

Sam gestured behind him with the eraser on his pencil. "Same scuff marks are on the window latch."

She drifted over to examine those as he went on.

"When he couldn't pop the window," Sam said, "he lost patience and punched through a couple of glass panes, which you had replaced." He indicated some slightly newer-looking glass panes. "Lucky for us, he cut himself doing it. I can see where you tried to get his blood out of the carpet. I say *he*, but it might have been a girl with big feet. What's left of the muddy footprint you mostly got out of the rug came from a man's 9½ or a woman's 11 shoe."

She stared at him quietly. "Anything else?" she asked, pouring herself some tea.

"Well, I think we can assume it's someone who's got a pretty personal beef with you," Sam said, "since they pissed in your teapot."

Ms. Lee gagged on her tea and recoiled, letting the cup and saucer crash onto her desk.

"Just joking," Sam said as he closed his notebook. "Which way's the infirmary?"

3

D&D

The planetarium was, by design, windowless. Its location, further, was at best vaguely known to anyone not in the astronomy club. This, combined with its proximity to two well-stocked vending machines (one of which sometimes gave up bonus Drake's cakes with a well-timed hip check), made it an ideal meeting place for the Dungeons & Dragons club (which overlapped with the astronomy club to a convenient degree).

Brad, Kapui and Niloofar studied a map. Harriet, the dungeon master, reviewed the hazards facing them behind a security screen. "You want to lose a level, Rob?" Harriet asked without looking up.

"Huh?" said Rob, who had drifted nonchalantly toward her flank.

"Try peeking at my notes again, I'm docking you one hundred thousand x.p."

Rob returned to the map, venting his pique on a bag of Fritos.

"At the base of the foothills is a towering pile of fist-size rocks," Harriet said. "Etched into each rock is a strange symbol."

"What do the symbols look like?" Niloofar asked.

"You pick up one of the rocks to examine it—" Harriet replied.

"Wait!" Kapui piped up. "She didn't say—"

"The symbol begins to glow, the rock becoming so hot you have to drop it," Harriet plowed on. "The symbol in every other rock in the pile begins to glow as well. Roll a dexterity check."

The party groaned, each rolling a twenty-sided die.

"I'm calling bullshit on that," Kapui griped.

"I'm getting tired of the whining," Harriet said. "Six D4 damage if you fail the check."

Kapui alone failed the roll. He pounded his head against the carpet. Niloofar offered him a plastic orc skull full of Junior Mints, but he would not be consoled.

"From the pile of rocks emerges what looks like a giant lizard made of fire," Harriet continued.

"A fucking salamander?" cried Brad.

"You wish," Harriet answered. "Hang on to your head-gear, Brad—this is a Balrog."

There were gasps, naturally, followed by an electric state of readiness.

"The demon brandishes its flaming whip," Harriet continued, "and—"

The room went dark. The club froze.

"What happened?" asked Brad.

Harriet felt her way to the light switch and juddered it. "Power's out," she said. She got a strong whiff of . . . melted fuse, maybe? But also leather, pine and camphor.

A pained moan from the corner.

"Rob?"

"Wasn't me."

A low growl from the back row. A hiss from near the fire exit.

"Who's in here?"

A scream from Niloofar.

"What's going on?" yelled Harriet.

A face, lit from below, bobbed near the audio console, snout and horns glistening. "You have summoned me and my minions from hell," it rasped. "You will pay for your blasphemy!"

Another face, lit from below, appeared by the projector, moaning and fanged.

A figure, by the chalkboard, wailed and lit something. "I cast a Protection Against Nerds spell!" The speaker lobbed a firecracker toward the middle of the map. The D&D club scattered to avoid the explosion. In the dark, Niloofar collided at full tilt with a Foucault pendulum. Its cymbal-like brang and her pained moans brought belly laughs from the intruders.

"*You assholes!*" Harriet shrieked. She wrenched Pluto off a solar-system model and hurled it at the largest of the assholes, who wagged his tongue luridly through a werewolf mask, a flashlight held below his chin. She reached for Neptune, intent on working her way to Mercury, when her body betrayed her. Her jaw locked, her limbs began to jerk, and she crashed to the ground.

"Fucking A," said the one in the werewolf mask, sweeping his flashlight over Harriet's convulsing body, "she's, like, totally spazzing out."

"She's having a seizure!" shrieked Niloofar. "Help her!"

Instead, the marauders fled, taking their flashlights with them.

"Harriet!" Niloofar yelled. "Oh, Jesus!"

"I'll get help!" Kapui said, feeling his way out the door.

"Hold her or something!" said Niloofar, who had followed the sound of Harriet's moaning and was forcing her sweater under Harriet's head to keep her from bashing it against the floor.

Rob and Brad found their way to Harriet and each grabbed a leg. Harriet's tremors slowed, then stopped. Everyone exhaled.

Then, as Rob would later describe it to Dr. O'Megaly, "Harriet just, like, freaked out."

He reported that Harriet had jackknifed into a sitting position, dazing Niloofar with a headbutt. Then Harriet "started saying these weird words really fast, but almost like if you played a record backward." And then she whipped one leg so forcefully that Brad left the floor and lost his right shoe before crashing into a row of chairs. "I let go at that point," Rob admitted, "and then Harriet did this like handspring thing and landed on top of the star projector. Which is like eight feet tall."

This could not be corroborated. And, as everyone admitted, the room had been dark.

4

THE INFIRMARY

A poster in the medical center read DON'T BE A BUTTHEAD! The poster showed a man with a cigarette filter for a head, crossed eyes and a large mouth with smoke billowing out through his gapped teeth. Sam fought the urge to strike a match against it and spark up a Kent.

He wasn't sure the high school he'd gone to had had a medical center. If it had, it had probably been one drawer in the teachers' lounge filled with aspirin and Band-Aids. This place was more like a small hospital. Now, true, they were a boat ride away from a major city, so they had to be able to handle some stuff, but damn: two stories, eighteen beds, a pharmacy, a full-time staff—

Yet no one had the time to talk to Sam.

"Dr. O'Megaly is with patients, but as soon as she has a moment, we'll let you know," the receptionist said.

"Can you tell her it's a little time sensitive but that I won't take long?" Sam asked.

"Sign in and we'll be with you as soon as we can," the receptionist answered in that irritating way receptionists have of not answering you.

Sam drummed his fingers on the desk in front of her for a moment, then went and sat. The Asian kid with the orange Mohawk was in the seat next to him. He didn't notice Sam at first, absorbed in whatever was pumping through his Walkman.

"What are you listening to?" Sam asked.

"The Germs," the kid said.

"They good?" Sam asked.

The kid shoved his earphones at Sam daringly. Sam put them on and heard the singer sputter something about a "lexicon devil" with a "battered brain."

Sam took the earphones off and politely returned them. "Sounds like they don't know how to play their instruments."

"They don't," said the kid. "Well, they didn't. Smear does. guess." Then he said defiantly, "It's punk, man. Sorry not everything's disco."

"Yeah, that's my scene," Sam said. "Disco."

"Not everyone wants to listen to stupid love songs all the time," the kid continued. "There's other stuff going on."

"I've heard," Sam said. "What brings you to the infirmary?"

"My tongue stud's infected," the kid said.

"Gross," Sam said. "Well, peer pressure's made me do stuff to myself, too." He extended his arm and showed the kid his tattoo of a snake wound about the words SEMPER FIDELIS. "My whole unit got these, snake and all."

"I didn't get this 'cause of peer pressure."

"I'm not judging you, kid. It's only natural to want to fit in. I mean, I *hope* it was peer pressure. Otherwise, you just like driving spikes into yourself. Also, I'd come clean to the doctor, I was you."

"Huh?" asked the kid.

"Your tongue stud's not infected," said Sam, "but judging by the way you keep wincing and shifting your weight, I'd guess the one in your pecker is."

The kid almost leapt out of his chair.

"All I'm saying is, you try to spare yourself some embarrassment by saying your tongue stud's infected in the hopes she gives you some antibiotics that work on your dick, suppose she gives you the wrong kind?" Sam asked. "You don't want them having to cut the thing off. Or maybe you do. Shit, you jammed metal through it, what do I know?"

"You were asking to see me?"

Sam looked up to see a brunette in a lab coat staring at him with her arms folded. Her silky brown bob curled under her chin and a few wisps on the right brushed her mouth. Sam envied them. She had plump lips, high cheekbones, olive skin and huge brown eyes flecked with fire. "You're Dr. Fran O'Megaly?" he asked.

"Yeah, and you're . . . ?"

"Sam Gregory," he said, standing and putting out his hand. "I'm an insurance investigator, here about that stolen book."

Dr. O'Megaly cocked her head. "Oh . . . from Ms. Lee's office?"

"That's it."

"What can I do for you?" the doctor asked.

"Just have a few questions, shouldn't take much time."

She sighed and looked at her watch. "I'm a little booked up, but if you don't mind sticking around for a half hour or so I can try to squeeze you in."

"No problem," Sam said, grabbing a magazine. "I can catch up on my *Weekly Readers*."

"Enjoy," the doctor said. "Haruki," she said, looking at the punk rocker, who quickly gathered his things and trotted after her. Haruki looked nervously back at Sam before he disappeared into one of the examination rooms. Sam gave him a thumbs-up and what he hoped would be interpreted as an encouraging smile. Despite his best efforts, Sam usually came across as snide even when he didn't mean to.

D r. O'Megaly paged through a folder. "Jock itch, ringworm, Osgood-Schlatter, water on the knee, flu, poison oak reaction, twisted ankle, pink eye, yeast infection and strep." She closed the folder. "No lacerations of any kind this week. Though, honestly, if I had stitched somebody up, I couldn't tell you who. Doctor-patient confidentiality and all that."

"Even if he cut himself committing a crime?" Sam asked.

She shrugged. "Kid walks in here with a bullet lodged in him, I gotta call the cops. Kid walks in showing obvious signs of abuse, I have to contact a social worker. Kid walks in pregnant, I need to inform the parents. Beyond that, for the most part, I'm supposed to keep my trap shut."

"Who do you call if a kid walks in pregnant, with a bullet wound, showing signs of abuse?" Sam asked.

"A career counselor," she said, brushing her hair back, "'cause I'm outta here. Nice tat." She nodded at his arm. "Youthful rebellion?"

"Rank conformity," Sam said, pulling back his sleeve to show the SEMPER FI, "my whole unit got them."

"Why'd you join the marines?" she asked.

"Youthful rebellion," he answered.

Amid several posters about the importance of hygiene and flossing and of avoiding drugs and sex, Sam's eyes fell on one with four concentric circles: red, blue, green and yellow. The yellow circle in the center had what looked like crosshairs over it and circumscribed the letters *NA*. Below it was a phone number. "There's a Narcotics Anonymous meeting here?" he asked.

"Yeah," said Dr. O'Megaly. "You looking for a meeting?"

Sam had lost a couple of years after he returned from Vietnam to all manner of controlled substances, and the recovery program at the VA came with a twelve-step. He stopped going when he couldn't take the higher-power bullshit any longer. Sam didn't know if there was a higher power, but if there was, it sure as hell didn't care what he was up to, and he resented pretending otherwise. "Just surprised to see this at a high school."

She shrugged. "Teenagers take drugs."

"School doesn't boot 'em out for that?" Sam asked.

"It does if they get caught. Not if they start going to meetings before that happens."

Sam bit his lip and looked at the poster again. He thought about the burglary: The guy has the combination. He can bide his time, wait for Ms. Lee to call in sick, leave her door unlocked when she goes to the can, give him some opening, but no. He busts through a glass window, doesn't even take enough precautions to avoid cutting himself, tracks blood and mud all over the carpet—that sounded like the reckless impatience of an addict. Sam knew it well. "Are outsiders welcome?"

Before she could answer, a gurney banged through the door. On it was a small Black girl with almost comically large glasses. Dr. O'Megaly gently lifted her lids and looked into her eyes with a penlight. Four students followed tentatively, one limping, another holding an ice pack to her face.

"Harriet?" Dr. O'Megaly said. "Harriet, honey, can you hear me?" Harriet, tears coursing lazily toward her ears, began to murmur. The doctor bent to hear as they entered an exam room. "Wait out here," she said to the four students with Harriet and shut the door.

Sam turned to the four. "What happened to her?"

"These jerks messed with us and she had a seizure," said a large, pale kid who was wearing a T-shirt with some math joke on it that Sam didn't understand.

"Who are you?" asked the girl holding the ice pack to her face.

"New student," Sam said, strolling out, "just transferred from Riverdale. Hope your friend feels better. See you at the sock hop."

5

THE FRIENDS OF BILL

On the chalkboard, someone had written YOU'RE ONLY AS SICK AS YOUR SECRETS. There was a Rubbermaid tub full of sodas at the back of the room and a tray of cookies. No coffee, which was unlike any other NA meeting Sam had ever attended, and no smoking either (the tolerance of which had been, for Sam, NA's most appealing feature).

The faculty moderator did not appear to be around, just a handful of fidgety teenagers sitting in folding chairs watching a handsome kid named Scott talk about rolling a tennis ball in weed so he could train his German shepherd to sniff out his stepbrother's stash.

A dry crunch drew everyone's attention to a plump, freckled kid with a mop of red hair who was biting into a stack of ten cookies. Scott stopped his sharing and addressed the red-head. "The cookies are for after, man."

"Sorry," said the redhead. His hand went out and back three times as he tried to decide whether to return the stack of cookies from which he'd taken a collective bite. In the end, he divided the spoils, returning half of the partly eaten cook-ies to the communal platter and jamming the other half into the pockets of his cargo shorts. Wrapped tightly around his right hand was a thick, filthy bandage.

The redhead brushed the crumbs off his tie-dyed T-shirt and took a seat in the back row next to a skinny blond kid with large, moist eyes who stared straight ahead with the in-tensity of a bomb defuser. Sam quietly moved to a seat behind them.

The redhead looked at the fidgety blond and smiled. "First meeting?" he whispered.

The blond kid darted him a surprised look, then laughed and nodded. The redhead smiled kindly. "We've all been there. Jimmy, by the way." He extended his good hand.

The blond kid shook it. "Edward," he said.

"How long you been clean?" Jimmy asked, fishing some broken cookies out of his cargo shorts.

"What time is it?" said Edward.

Jimmy chuckled with an understanding nod. "Why'd you quit?"

"Don't want to get expelled," Edward explained.

"Yeah, yeah." Jimmy nodded. "What's your thing?"

"Uh . . . weed, mostly," Edward answered.

"No kidding?" Jimmy said, looking around and edging a little closer. "'Cause, um, I got the sweetest hookup."

"Huh?" said Edward.

"Expensive, but totally worth it," Jimmy explained. "And not expensive at all for how good it is. I can get you a half ounce for—"

F orty-five seconds later, Jimmy was bodily ejected from the building.

"Jesus, I was just joking!" Jimmy said. "Would you guys relax?"

Scott shoved Jimmy in the chest, causing him to stagger backward and sit on the cookies in his rear pocket. Scott pointed at Jimmy's bandaged hand and said, "Come to this meeting again and the rest of you is going to need bandages."

"Wow, you know, nice," said Jimmy. "Maybe you should look into a program for your rage issues."

"I'm telling Mr. Forester, you fat shithead," said Scott.

"And I'll tell him you assaulted me," said Jimmy, "you twelve-step fascist prick."

Several fuck-yous volleyed back and forth before Scott and the rest of the faithful went back inside. Jimmy got to his feet and loped away muttering to himself. So preoccupied was he by his wound licking and revenge fantasies that he walked right into Sam and bounced off him. "Jesus," Jimmy said.

"Not even close," replied Sam.

Jimmy stared at Sam, puzzled, and looked around for some qualifying presence: a tour group, a work crew, anything to provide a context for this buff, scary-looking guy with a crew cut. He found none. "Yeah, well . . . whatever, man," Jimmy said and bustled past Sam. To Jimmy's chagrin, Sam followed.

"You're lucky you tried that crap in a meeting for private-school kids," Sam said. "Anywhere else, a couple of Hells Angels would be stomping on you right now, arguing over who got to keep your teeth."

Jimmy snuck a glance over his shoulder at Sam and quickened his pace. "Yeah, well, I don't know you or what you think you heard, but there was a misunderstanding. And that meeting's confidential anyhow, so how 'bout you stop following me now and go about your business of whatever the hell you're doing here and leave me alone."

"How'd you hurt your hand?" Sam asked.

"Punching some weirdo who wouldn't leave me alone," Jimmy said. "Look, I don't know if you're gay, or crazy, or what, but I'm not—"

Sam caught up to Jimmy, grabbed his index finger, and with no perceivable effort twisted him into a painful joint lock. Jimmy gasped and fell to his knees. Sam peeked under the bandage on his hand. "Hmmm . . . Nah . . . You punched somebody wrong, you might hurt your wrist or your fingers. It wouldn't slice your hand like that. You slashed this on something jagged, like glass."

"Help! I don't know this guy! Help!" Jimmy yelled. But except for a few birds that kept merrily chirping, they were alone on the wooded path behind the meeting hall.

"You hear about this burglary the other day?" Sam asked casually. "Somebody smashed through a window in the library and made off with a real valuable book. Looked like they cut themselves. Also, they had shoes your size."

Jimmy stopped wriggling and froze. "So fucking what? It wasn't me."

"Well, that's a shame 'cause I'd give you five hundred bucks for it," Sam said. "No questions asked."

Jimmy twisted his head up to look at Sam. Sam's face was upside down from Jimmy's inverted position, his grin twisted into a toothy frown. "Sure you would," Jimmy said. "You a cop?"

"Nope, I work for the insurance company," said Sam. "And that's super lucky for you because it means I don't give a shit about anything but getting that book back. It ends up in my hands, the person who got it there gets half a grand, end of story."

Sam released Jimmy who stood and staggered sideways,

taking his shoulder into a brick wall. He swore and rubbed his shoulder and shook out his hand, but he didn't run. He just stared at Sam. "Jesus, you, like, sincerely messed up my finger. I should sue your ass."

"Good luck," Sam said as he began writing down the room and phone number for his guest quarters on a business card. "I get the book back, you get the money, I leave. I don't get the book back, you don't get the money, I keep hanging around here seeing all sorts of stuff that I may or may not tell the cops about. And they're not interested in making you any richer." Sam stuffed the business card between the cookie crumbs in one of Jimmy's pockets. "This offer expires at midnight."

6

THE FOURTH ESTATE

I diopathic generalized epilepsy was how doctors had labeled Harriet's neurological disorder. Epilepsy, though an ancient disease, isn't particularly well understood. Idiopathic, meaning "of unknown origin," simply underscored the fact that Harriet's condition baffled her physicians. All anyone really knew was that stress seemed to trigger seizures involving very forceful muscle contractions that, when they finally subsided, left her spent and foggy.

As she had had a seizure only this morning, the fact that she was now brimming with energy and laser-like focus was something of a miracle. This miracle was lost on Mr. Chesterton, Harriet's journalism teacher, who had been looking forward to a quiet lunch doing the crossword when his most demanding student had barreled into his office. In the ten minutes she'd been talking, Mr. Chesterton did not think he'd seen her inhale.

"They need to be exposed," Harriet said. "This is about the fourth estate doing its goddamned job."

Mr. Chesterton winced and patted his belly. "Let's clean up the talk, shall we? Also, I don't think chasing down pranksters is the job of the school paper."

"Pranksters?" She slapped the desk so hard, his pencil holder trembled. "I had a seizure!"

"I know—"

"Brad's ear is still ringing from a firecracker exploding next to it. Is that a cute little joke?"

"No, my point is that campus security—"

"*Campus security* is a cute little joke! They still haven't found out who crapped in Josh Beckman's sousaphone!"

Mr. Chesterton grimaced. "Someone . . . what?"

"He realized it during the halftime show and threw up four notes into 'Smoke on the Water'!"

"I . . . This is the first I'm hearing this story."

"Because no one cares! Because when jocks at this school torment kids like me, everyone thinks it's just hilarious!"

"I don't."

"Then let me write an exposé on bullying and jock culture at Danforth Putnam. Let me nail these sons of bitches."

Mr. Chesterton sighed and looked longingly at the bologna sub Harriet had delayed him from unwrapping, an ice-cold can of Tab beading invitingly next to it.

"Can't you just write the five hundred words on Hello Day I asked for?" he groaned.

"Hello Day," Harriet spat. "I don't know what's more embarrassing: the historical inaccuracies about Pilgrims meeting what they still unbelievably refer to as Indians, the shoddy production values, the cringeworthy performances, or that they seem to confuse singing with yelling."

"They're fifth graders."

Harriet folded her hands prayerfully and tapped her forehead against her knuckles. She squeezed her eyes shut and blew into the gap beneath her thumbs. "Mr. Chesterton, if you'd been there . . ."

She pictured Niloofar, her first friend at Danforth Putnam, groaning in the pit beneath the Foucault pendulum, one of those apes kicking sand in her hair. She saw Rob searching for his glasses, slapped off by another of those thugs; Kapui, shoved to the ground and forced to watch as they stomped on the figurines he'd spent hours painting—three of them for Harriet's birthday; Brad trying to crawl under a desk while they pelted him with dice; those goons bent over with laughter, hugging themselves.

Harriet did not consider herself a vengeful person (this

was a blind spot because the truth was she had never forgotten a slight in her life), but how could she possibly let this go unanswered?

"Mr. Chesterton, all I'm asking you to do is care. All I'm asking is that, for once, you remember you're a damn newsman, and let me do my job."

Mr. Chesterton ran both hands up over his face and through his thinning hair, which he then gripped for dear life. He stared at Harriet, wide-eyed, then glanced pleadingly at his sandwich as though it might weigh in on his behalf. When it did not, he sighed, defeated.

"If you give me five hundred words on Hello Day, which aren't unpublishably vitriolic, I'll look at a feature on campus bullying. But I am not printing anything that isn't fair and thoroughly sourced. And you definitely do not have my permission to do anything illegal, unethical or against school policy. Understood?"

"Understood," Harriet said with a slow and pointed wink.

Mr. Chesterton frowned. "See, that wink makes me think you believe I've given you some sort of tacit permission to—"

"I won't let you down, Mr. Chesterton," Harriet said, grabbing her backpack and heading for the door.

"Do not break any . . ." were the last words Harriet could make out from Mr. Chesterton, who, she knew, had neither the energy nor the will to follow her down the stairs.

7

DALE

The soccer field was ablaze with the lowering autumn sun. From the shadows amid a rise of white pines behind the bleachers, Dale watched the players dart and kick. He was particularly interested in this scrimmage because he'd hurled a few pinecones onto the field before practice. He saw a forward step on one and collapse, clutching his ankle. He smiled.

For as long as he'd been at Danforth Putnam, Dale had been told how lucky he was. This place had been his home since his father had fallen asleep in a drunken stupor on the sofa with a cigarette in his mouth, started a fire and killed everyone in the family but Dale. He'd been nine years old, with sixty percent of his body covered in burn scars, his whole family charred like roasted marshmallows, and all anyone ever told him was how incredibly lucky he was. Lucky to scrub the toilets, mop the floors, bus the trays, wash the dishes and all but wipe the asses of the rich little pricks here who were too good for that sort of thing.

One of those little pricks was sitting across from him.

Craig, he said his name was. He was fifteen, allegedly, but looked twelve. His short hair was plastered to the sides and he wore a crisp Oxford shirt, dress pants and penny loafers, all of which were too big for him. He looked like a forty-year-old who'd been zapped with some magic ray that made him a little kid again but left his clothes and hair all grown up.

"It's the statement you want to make about yourself as a man," Dale told him. He saw Craig give a little nod. The kid liked someone referring to him as a man. "The choice you make, it says something," Dale went on, opening his eyes wide and inclining his head as if he were sharing something important with this kid. "Says something to your peers, says something to you. Now . . ."

Dale took a quarter-ounce bag of pot out of his backpack. "This is the Toyota Corolla. Nothing wrong with the Corolla, it's reliable, it'll get you where you want to go, but it's going to be an uneventful ride and will impress no one."

Dale took out another quarter-ounce bag of pot and placed it next to the first. "This is the Beemer. Smooth, clean, a cut above the Corolla to be sure. But then there's . . ."

With palpable reverence, Dale lifted a third quarter-ounce

bag from his backpack and placed it lovingly next to the other two. "The Ferrari. Some men can't handle all that speed and power, but for the ones who can, this says something about them. It says confidence. It says only the best for them. And girls . . . wow . . . you take a girl on this ride with you . . ." He broke into an intense whisper. "You won't be able to pry her off you with a stick."

Craig licked his lips and swallowed. "How much?"

"Fifty," Dale answered.

"I got thirty-five," said Craig.

"The Beemer's good," Dale said, chucking the other two bags into his backpack.

As Craig reached for his wallet, the sound of twigs snapping and something lumbering toward them through the woods brought the exchange to a halt.

"Hey, buddy," Jimmy said.

"Shit!" Craig said and bolted off like a frightened deer, leaving behind one of his penny loafers, but not, Dale noted with disappointment, any of his money.

Dale leapt to his feet and gave Jimmy a shove. "The fuck are you doing?" he shouted.

Jimmy staggered back, his hands held high. "What? Sorry. Didn't mean to scare the kid." He laughed.

Dale didn't. "What do you want?" he asked.

"Um . . ." Jimmy rubbed his thighs and looked around. "I was wondering if I could get that thing back from you."

"What thing?"

"That . . . that book you wanted me to get," Jimmy mumbled.

Dale blinked at Jimmy for a few seconds, then smiled. "Why would you wonder that?"

"It's just . . . people are looking for it now," Jimmy said.

Dale straightened, looked around and got a little closer to Jimmy. "What people?" he asked quietly.

"Just, you know, word's out that it was stolen, and I think we should give it back before we get into some serious trouble," Jimmy explained.

"Ah," said Dale. "And are we planning to give me back the weed I gave you to get it for me?"

"Well, I mean . . . Look, a guy from the insurance company said he'd give me two hundred bucks for it," Jimmy said.

"What?" Dale asked, his voice dropping an octave.

"I'll totally split it with you," Jimmy said quickly.

"You told some guy you stole it?" Dale asked.

"No, he just thinks I stole it," Jimmy answered.

"Why?" Dale asked.

"I don't know," Jimmy said, "but he said if I give it to him—look, he's not a cop, he doesn't give a shit, he just wants the book back. He said it's like, he gets the book, he's gone, no one's in trouble, we just get two hundred dollars."

Dale stared at Jimmy for a long time, then smiled. "Sweet," he said.

"I mean, not bad, right?" Jimmy said, encouraged.

"I can never quite believe how stupid you are," Dale said.

"What?" said Jimmy.

"You honestly believe that?" Dale asked with quiet wonder. "You honestly believe you're going to be like 'Oh, yeah, sure, I busted into the library and stole this shit. Here. Where's my money?' How brain-damaged are you?"

"Look, what do you want the damn thing for, anyway?" asked Jimmy.

"Why, gosh, I don't see that's your business, James," Dale said and took a step closer to Jimmy. "Did you give him my name?"

"No," said Jimmy, shuffling backward.

"Good," said Dale. "Hey, are you taking European History?"

Jimmy stared at him. "I think so."

"Only class I'm doing good in," Dale said. "I think it's the violence." He chuckled and gave Jimmy a friendly swat on the shoulder. "What does that say about me?"

Jimmy tried to chuckle along. "I don't know."

"Do you know what the legal punishment for treason was in England until 1870? The legal one?"

"No."

Dale rolled his eyes. "Buddy . . . go to class once in a while. Drawing and quartering."

"Cool."

"Cool?" Dale said, stepping closer and closer to Jimmy. "Do you know what they did? They slowly pulled your intestines out. While you were alive. I mean . . . that's taking betrayal pretty personally."

Jimmy had, by now, backed up against a tree and was nearly nose to nose with Dale. "Jesus Christ," Jimmy whispered, "you don't have to be psycho about this. Forget I said anything."

Dale stared into Jimmy's eyes for a few seconds, then smiled and stepped back. "I don't know what you mean, Jim. We're just talking. Friends, right? Here." He unzipped his backpack and tossed Jimmy a bag of weed. "On the house."

Jimmy stared at Dale warily. Dale smiled magnanimously and delicately swept the air with the back of his hand in a gesture of dismissal. Jimmy shook his head and crunched back off through the woods the way he'd come, examining the bag of pot. "Oh, man, the Corolla?" Jimmy muttered as he disappeared.

Dale smiled as his eyes caught the last orange kiss of the sun and he thought about this place and everyone in it burning. The soccer practice in the distance was disbanding, the embers of the fall foliage cooling as the sun vanished and the field joined Dale in shadow.

Dale smelled him before he saw him. How did he apply that gross aftershave? Did he sit in a bathtub full of it? Whatever the answer, Dale was grateful for the warning. Not that he feared Paul. He just didn't like anyone being able to sneak up on him. Paul was surprisingly quiet for such a big guy. He hulked in the shadows, staring at Dale.

Dale wordlessly opened his pack and handed Paul a small cooler. Paul wordlessly examined the contents, handed Dale a wad of cash and turned to go.

"I might need some mouths shut," Dale said.

Paul slowly turned back toward Dale, alert but impassive, a golem awaiting its violent writ.

8

MICHAEL

They did what?" Michael asked when Harriet described the assault on the D&D club. He laughed so hard that she thought he might choke on his Salisbury steak. If he did, she wasn't sure she'd speed to his rescue. She did not inform him that she'd been among those terrorized or that she was writing an article about it for the school paper. Instead, she just grinned wanly and did her best to seem as tickled by the attack as he was.

Josh Beckman had told Harriet that he was certain a football player had defiled his sousaphone, though he did not know which one. The D&D club assailants had been large and jocky and clearly delighted in humiliating nerds, so

Harriet wondered if there was some overlap between Josh's aggressors and her own.

There were only six Black students at Danforth Putnam. One of them, Michael, was on the football team. Michael was the only football player Harriet knew, and this only vaguely, because they had both attended a "minority mixer" some gratingly well-intentioned (and White) faculty member had organized. During the fifteen minutes Harriet had lasted at this painful affair, she and Michael had nodded at each other over punch, acknowledging that, yes, they were both, indeed, Black. Beyond this, they could find nothing in common.

Still, he was the only even tenuous connection Harriet had to the football team, so she contrived to run into him in the dining hall at the tail end of dinner. Now Michael guffawed so convulsively at what had befallen the D&D club, he gagged on his Fanta, his eyes watering. "They get in trouble?"

"They haven't been caught," Harriet replied. "I wonder if it's the same people who did that thing to Josh Beckman's sousaphone."

He grew quiet and frowned into his soda. "Those guys are messed up."

"You know them?" she asked, trying to look absorbed in opening a bag of mini-pretzels.

Michael squirmed in his seat. "I mean, I'm not really in with them. They're . . . they're into some stuff."

"Stuff?" Harriet asked, studying a pretzel before popping it into her mouth.

"Bad stuff. Worse than crapping in tubas."

"Wow."

"I mean, we're teammates, right? And I want to stay cool with them, because I don't want them feeling like maybe they shouldn't work so hard at blocking for me."

Harriet nodded and wished, for the first time in her life, that she knew something about football, specifically who blocked for whatever it was Michael did.

"You're the quarterback?" she asked.

"No, running back. But those guys, one in particular . . ." Michael leaned forward, his eyes flitting around the dining hall. "Dude is scary. What he's into . . . I mean, it's definitely dangerous, probably illegal and . . ." He froze, his eyes on Harriet's bag.

"What is?" Harriet asked.

Michael plunged his hand into her bag and withdrew a mini tape recorder, the reels of which were quietly spinning. He thrust it at her.

"What the hell is this?" he asked.

"That's for . . . class," Harriet stammered, flushing. "I use it to take notes—"

"Why's it on?"

"It got bumped around in my bag, I guess. I—"

Michael pulled out the tape, pocketed it and chucked the

tape recorder back in Harriet's bag. He gathered his things and spoke without looking at her.

"I don't know you, I didn't say anything and I don't know anything. Don't talk to me again."

"Michael, I . . ." she began lamely, but he was already out the door.

H arriet asked her friends in the D&D club if they knew who "blocked" for a "running back." None of them did, so she went to the library and looked up football.

Her reading didn't improve Harriet's opinion of the game. Even its name represented an act of bullying, as the game had stolen it from another sport (one for which *foot ball* actually made sense) and forced that sport to go by *soccer* instead. She took a long detour, during her research, into the Carlisle Indian Industrial School, 1879 through 1918, which had plucked young Native American boys off reservations and attempted to assimilate them into White society with cheerful adages like "Kill the Indian, Save the Man." Their football team was coached by Pop Warner, an early innovator of the game, at a time when—unbelievably—it was even more violent. In 1905, when it was still largely a school sport (a professional league wouldn't form for another fifteen years), 19 boys died and another 137 were critically injured playing football. That was one season.

She deduced that those tasked with blocking for Michael were aptly referred to as "offensive linemen." After combing through the sports pages from the school paper, she learned that there were ten offensive linemen on the DP Puritans varsity roster, but that the star player was named Paul Spitz.

The most intriguing thing Harriet found had never been printed. It was a galley proof of an article by Matt Kuhn, last year's student editor, who was now at Dartmouth. It was a profile on Paul and detailed how he had massively increased in size since his sophomore year, broken several athletic records and already had the eye of Division I college coaches.

It also mentioned Paul Spitz's temper, which had caused more than one bench clearer. A particularly notable one ensued at an away game in Taunton after Paul felt mocked by Andrew Cowan, a safety from the other team. Following the game, an assailant wearing a Halloween mask ambushed Cowan outside the Taunton locker room and beat him so savagely that he ended up in the hospital with career-ending injuries. Cowan believed that Spitz was the attacker but police were declining to investigate him because Spitz's grandfather was a close friend of the Massachusetts governor, Edward King (a former offensive lineman with the Buffalo Bills and Baltimore Colts). Mr. Chesterton had drawn a large red *X* through this section next to the question "Libel?" so it never made the paper.

Harriet decided to have a look around Paul's room.

9

JIMMY'S CALL

*H*ot. So hot. Hard to believe it's planet Earth. Shit, maybe it isn't. How can it be raining and this hot? Sommers is screaming at a kid. Farmer. Maybe fourteen. Frozen, staring at Sommers, his mouth wide open, too scared to drop the basket he's holding. Sommers has his M16 in the kid's face, keeps screaming at him to drop the basket, but it's not like the kid knows English, Woods says. Woods tries to pull Sommers off, and now it's a fight, but Cooper finds it funny for some reason. Then the flash of something metal across the river. Half of Sommers's face explodes in a frothy pink-and-white mist and a giant red blossom opens across the front of Lieberstein's pants and Lieberstein screams. I hit the dirt and the kid takes a grenade out of the basket and pulls the pin as I leave a smoking hole in his forehead and he arches in a *backward swan dive as the grenade rolls from his hand and explodes in a geyser of mud and limbs and Cooper shouts into a radio and then the earth caves in and I'm swimming in midair, falling toward a horizonless ocean of orange magma and—*

S am flinched upright at the sound of the phone on his nightstand ringing. He wiped the sweat off his face and hands and scrambled for the receiver.

"Sam Gregory."

He heard someone breathing on the other end of the line, then the rustle of a bag, the crunching of chips and the hollow gurgle of what sounded like a bong. Eventually, the caller exhaled and whispered, "Come on, answer."

"I did answer," Sam said.

He heard the clatter of the phone being dropped and picked up again.

"What?" the caller said. "Hello? Somebody there?"

"This is Sam Gregory. Can I help you?"

"Oh, hey, it's Jimmy Fossor. You're the guy from today with . . . outside the . . . You grabbed my fingers?"

"Evening, Jimmy."

"I was thinking about your offer. The one you said expires at midnight?"

Sam looked at the clock radio by his bed. "It's 2:05."

"Really? Shit."

"You have the book?"

"No, but I know who does," Jimmy said.

"Who?" Sam asked.

"I still get the money, right?" Jimmy asked. "I mean, I tell you where it is, that's pretty much like handing it to you, right?"

"If it's where you say it is and I get it without any hassle, sure, the money's yours," Sam said. "So, who has it?"

"You can't tell him I told you, though, right? 'Cause we're sort of friends and he's, like, really crazy."

"Fine. Who are we talking about?"

"The guy I gave the book to," Jimmy answered impatiently. "Are you even listening to me?"

Sam took several breaths before saying anything. "For the fourth fucking time, Jim, what's his name?"

"Dale. Lauferson. He's in Hastings House 314."

Sam flipped open his notebook and wrote it down. "Why'd you give him the book?"

"He wanted it, I don't know why. He won't tell me. You said no questions asked."

"Pretty sure I said something about putting it in my hands. You're just giving me an address," Sam said. "That entitles me to a few questions. Like why'd you give him the book?"

"He said he'd give me some pot if I boosted it for him. I did. And that's all I know. Seriously. I don't know anything else. When do I get paid?"

"I'll check him out in the morning. If I get the book, you get your money."

"Why don't you check him out now?"

"'Cause it's 2:07."

"Really? Shit."

"Good night, Jimmy."

Sam hung up and unplugged the phone. He lay wide-eyed on the twin bed of the room they'd given him and stared at the ceiling. After twenty minutes of that, he got out of bed and opened the Dopp kit tied inside two sweaters and buried at the bottom of his duffel. From the panoply of grade A pharmaceuticals within, he selected a combination of meds he'd found effective of late, downed them and got back into bed. He was no longer dosing strictly as directed and this did occasionally give him pause, but he reminded himself that he was not after a recreational mood swing. He was just after sleep. He was just after slowing his mind to the point where his thoughts did not race violently and vividly from image to image, but drifted lazily: like vapor, like clouds, like feathers in a breeze, like notes from harp strings plucked with fingers made of starlight. . . .

10

JIMMY'S ROOM

Jimmy hung up the phone, took the bag of pot Dale had given him (now considerably lighter), sifted through some of it on top of a Spanish grammar workbook with a creaseless spine and did another bowl. Even through the mellow from his nicely decelerated neurons, he was beginning to wonder if calling that cop dude had been such a hot idea.

But you know what, screw Dale, he thought. Jimmy had tried to do right by him, give him a heads-up, split most of the money with him, but Dale had decided he was some sort of badass, stepping to him in the woods and talking a bunch of shit about pulling his intestines out. To hell with that guy.

As long as he could remember, Jimmy had taken crap from people. Whether it was his mom making fun of his "shit-brown eyes," his older brother lifting his shirt up and jiggling his belly in front of everyone at Sebago Lake (that hot girl from the Clanderson family he'd had a crush on nearly pissed her tennis whites she was laughing so hard), Señor Jiménez stapling his puka shell necklace to the desk when he fell asleep in Spanish class (a teacher did that!), those self-righteous dickheads at NA, that cop dude . . .

But Dale? Who the hell was Dale? If they knew for one second the stuff Dale was up to, if Jimmy breathed one word of it, Dale would be out on his ass and where the hell would that be? He had no family, so what did that leave? Juvie? The street? And he thought he could get in Jimmy's face like that? Well, fuck that guy. Fuck him twice. Fuck him, eat him and shit him out like the turd he was.

Jimmy took another bong hit and sat down to study. Yes, study. Maybe everybody thought he didn't care about his grades, but he did. There was a quiz tomorrow in biology and he intended to get an A. He uncrumpled the test results he'd paid ten bucks for and started to memorize the answers: A, C, D, A, D, A, B, B, B . . .

There was a loud thump. Jimmy looked up. No more thumps followed, however, so he returned his attention to the test answers.

After a moment, though, there was another thump. It came from his closet. Jimmy threw his pot into a desk drawer and opened the closet door.

On the floor of the closet was a large heap of clothes. To his horror, the heap was moving. Jimmy closed the door, put his back to it and tried to think. He was entirely unsure of how to proceed. He didn't know why his clothes had suddenly started to move, wasn't even completely sure he'd seen what he thought he saw, but he was pretty sure that he should investigate further. He grabbed a lacrosse stick, reopened the closet door and visually confirmed that the heap of clothes was indeed moving. Not much, just a little, but it was slowly pulsing up and down as if it were breathing. Jimmy choked up as far as he could on the lacrosse stick and gingerly prodded at the heap. He missed with the first two prods but connected with the third.

Something lashed out of the heap with a yowl. Jimmy jumped back, one foot landing in a wastepaper basket, and clattered to the floor, crushing a ukulele.

Ms. Lee's cat, Crowley, stared at him.

"The hell are you doing here?" Jimmy said and then paused, as though genuinely expecting a response. "Get out of my room!" He threw the mangled ukulele at Crowley. The cat darted out of the way, turned to growl at him, then hissed and jumped out of Jimmy's window.

Jimmy shook the wastepaper basket from his foot, stood up and closed the window.

The encounter with Crowley was killing his buzz in a way he did not appreciate. He locked the window, double-checked that he'd locked it, unlocked it thinking he was locking it, then double-checked and locked it again. He went through the same routine with his door, then went back to his window, and was back at his room door again when he heard a scraping sound coming from his bathroom: claws on tile.

"Who the fuck's in there?"

No one answered. Jimmy grabbed the lacrosse stick and tiptoed toward the bathroom. He took a few deep breaths, then lunged inside with a war whoop.

Shielding his face, he flailed about with the lacrosse stick like a musketeer slashing at opponents on all sides. After dashing most of his toiletries into the sink and ripping a World Series of Rock poster above his john, he opened his eyes but kept the lacrosse stick raised and ready.

He saw that the shower curtain was closed. He girded himself with a few more deep breaths and then batted at the curtain until it opened.

The tub was empty, but the faucet was leaking; its slow, echoing splat was the noise that had drawn him in. He twisted the tap shut and noticed that the window above the tub was open. He looked out the window, saw nothing but an empty roof, slammed the window shut and locked it.

He was about to leave the bathroom and make sure he'd locked his room door again when something in the toilet caught his eye. It appeared to be a writhing snake. Jimmy was shuffling out of the bathroom, his back pressed against the wall farthest from the toilet, like a mountain climber on a six-inch ledge, when he realized that the thing in the toilet wasn't moving. Nor was it a snake but merely his electric razor knocked into the toilet during his assault. He took the razor out of the john and stared at its vaguely fang-like blades, its cord twisted behind it like a tail. He beheld the razor like an archaeologist studying a shard of Sumerian pottery just pulled from a dig, tilting it this way and that and watching, fascinated, as water spilled from its innards. "I got to stop partying," he told the razor.

He would not get the chance. The bathroom door creaked open, and before Jimmy could look up, something had opened him from love handle to love handle. He tried to keep his intestines from spooling out with his hands while that something lifted him and sent him crashing into the tub. He clawed his way to his feet, his face pressed against the window above his tub, as he was slashed again and again and again.

The last thing he saw, perched on the roof outside his window like a gargoyle locked in permanent witness, was Dale.

11

TRICK OR TREAT

It was one of those crisp, cloudless, late-October mornings in New England that clarifies all the appeal of the place. It made people want to go apple picking, visit cider mills, play touch football and jump into leaf piles, and it made Sam want to swallow his gun and accentuate the vibrant colors of the foliage with his brain matter. The energy of the rosy-cheeked children crunching over brilliant red dogwood leaves, the smell of split maple tree logs and balsam firs, the bracing chill, the crystal-clear air: It all set his teeth on edge. A silent, wan figure, marching across the quad in a long dark coat, combat boots and sunglasses, a cigarette clenched in his lipless frown, he felt like a creature of the underworld, sent by death on some terrible errand to this ghastly realm of sunshine and life, and no more comfortable in it than a snail in a salt mine.

It had been a bad night. Despite the meds, he kept waking up in cold sweats, more and more of the bedding flung wildly by his thrashing, until finally at about 4 a.m., he snapped awake, his pulse about one-twenty, on a completely denuded mattress. He gave up on sleep after that.

Once the sun was up, he showered, dressed and headed to the cafeteria.

"ID?" the cashier said.

He didn't even slow down. Just hopped the turnstile, ignored the cashier's monotone threat to call security, wordlessly filled a twenty-two-ounce soda cup with coffee and left.

Sam's mood wasn't improved by running into Ms. Lee outside the cafeteria.

"You're up early," she said as if she were accusing him of something.

"Well, my day's never right unless I get to paint the sunrise," Sam said. "You know a kid named Dale Lauferson?"

Ms. Lee rolled her eyes. "Dale didn't steal the book."

"Why do you say that?" Sam asked.

"Because he was working," she explained. "A faculty party at the headmaster's house. I saw him and so did two dozen other teachers. He was there the whole evening."

"You mean, as far as anyone can remember," Sam said

with a knowing smile. "I have to assume that once Ms. Lee shows up to a party, things get rock 'n' roll cuh-ray-zay." He winked and sauntered off across the quad looking for the address Jimmy had given him.

He didn't at first notice the figures breathing heavily into masks stalking him. As they drew closer, though, he felt them and turned.

Six ten-year-olds stood before him. Each wore a grotesque papier-mâché mask and a black cloak. Each cloak had a different word stenciled across the back: GLUTTONY, PRIDE, LUST, SLOTH, ENVY and GREED.

Pride strode up to Sam. He took a giant chocolate bar out of a shopping bag and thrust it at Sam like a priest trying to subdue a vampire with a crucifix. "Would you like to buy some chocolate?"

Sam stared slack-jawed at this confusing tableau. "Huh?"

"We're trying to raise money for our play," the boy said, "*The Seven Deadly Sins.*"

"Oh. Uh . . . I try not to eat chocolate. Sugar's bad for you."

"Cigarettes are bad for you," Gluttony said.

"Yeah, well, you kids start selling cigarettes, I'm in," Sam said. "Can you tell me where Hastings House 314 is?"

"Yes," said Pride. "Are you sure you don't want to buy some chocolate, sir?"

They stared at each other. Sam sighed and got out his wallet. "Shaken down by ten-year-olds. That's staying out of the report."

Pride took Sam's money, handed him a giant chocolate bar and pointed to a redbrick building a hundred feet away next to a clock tower. "That one. Room 314's on the third floor."

"Thanks," said Sam. "Hey, where's the seventh?"

"Seventh what?" asked Sloth.

"Sin," said Sam.

"Missing," said Lust.

"Missing?" said Sam.

"Our friend Izzy. Nobody can find him," Greed said.

"He might have run away," said Envy.

"Run away where? You're on an island," Sam said. "You tell your teachers this?"

"Yeah," said Pride. "They said—"

The boy's head jerked back and a hole opened in the forehead of his mask.

Sam whirled around looking for the shooter.

The boy staggered but did not fall. He shook off the blow and removed his mask. A welt was rising just below his hairline. He looked at the mask, saw the hole right between the eyes and began to scream.

From a window on the third floor of Hastings House, Sam spotted the glint of an air rifle.

"Hey!" Sam shouted toward the window.

The rifle disappeared. In seconds, Sam had darted into the entryway and was charging up the steps.

Sam burst into a dorm room and saw the tall, skinny kid with the Ronald Reagan button he'd seen get slapped the day he arrived. The kid was affecting such intense, eye-popping absorption in the textbook he was reading that he couldn't be bothered to look up when a strange man slammed open his door so forcefully that it bounced off the wall. The kid was six-foot-three easy but looked to weigh no more than one hundred twenty pounds. He wore a dark suit so short that Sam could see an inch of painfully white calf peeking out over each of his argyle socks. His hair had what looked to be some sort of industrial grease in it and was angrily slicked over his forehead to cover a large constellation of acne.

"The hell's wrong with you!" Sam roared at him.

"Who are you? What are you doing in my room?" the kid said.

"Are you fucking nuts? You almost put that kid's eye out!" Sam shouted.

"You know, I don't appreciate that language. But I didn't shoot at those kids who were unharmed and deserved it anyway," the kid said, licking his index finger and turning a page so violently that he almost tore it from the book.

"Give me the BB gun," Sam said.

"How dare you?" said the kid. "I don't know who you are. I didn't invite you into my room. Now please leave before—"

Sam caught the kid around his very prominent Adam's apple and lifted him out of the chair. He locked eyes with him as the kid sputtered and gagged and tried to pry loose Sam's fingers, his face purpling and his eyeballs straining in their sockets. "Give. Me. The. Gun."

Sam dropped the kid back into his chair. The kid gasped and tried to get to his feet. Sam leaned into him and the kid thought better of standing. The kid grabbed an air rifle from under his desk and threw it at Sam. "Here! Maniac."

Sam caught it by the barrel and planted the butt on the ground at parade rest.

"Who are you?" asked the kid.

"I'm a detective for an insurance company," Sam said. "Know anything about a rare book, just got stolen?"

The kid pressed his glasses up the bridge of his nose and folded his arms. "I'd like to see some identification, please."

Sam raised the air rifle and shot the kid in the kneecap. The kid pitched forward, his mouth open in a silent howl, and began rubbing the hole in his dress pants.

"Know anything about a rare book, just got stolen?"

"No!" the kid squealed.

"What's your name?" asked Sam.

"Charles . . . Dunder . . . man," said the kid.

"I'm in your room. I can find out your name," said Sam.

"Bernard Sandoval," said the kid.

"You know Dale Lauferson?" asked Sam.

"He lives across the hall," said Bernard.

Sam crossed the hallway and rapped on the door. There was no answer and the door was locked.

"Any idea where your buddy Dale is?" asked Sam, returning to Bernard's room.

"He is *not* . . ." Bernard said, whipping over a page of his book for emphasis, "my buddy."

"Why's that?" asked Sam.

"Because he's a menace," answered Bernard, "because he constantly uses my prescription face soap even though he says he doesn't, he's always painting penises on my scholarship awards and he keeps buying chocolate from those little monsters and leaving it in plain sight just because he knows I have a medical condition that forbids me from eating it."

"He buys chocolate from little kids?" Sam said. "Wow, the guy does sound like a dick."

"He shouldn't even be here," Bernard announced into his book.

"Why's that?"

"He's one of the charity cases like those animals selling chocolate down there."

"Dale's one of the foster kids here?"

"They don't pay and that jacks up the tuition for the rest of us."

"Your parents having trouble swinging your tuition, Bernie?"

"No, and it's Bernard, and it's just . . . it's . . . I don't see why *we* have to pay for *them*. Sorry to break it to you, but the sixties are over! Your generation may have wrecked the country with orgies and drugs and sit-ins and all that bleeding-heart hippie crap, but we believe in responsibility now."

"So you looked at this haircut and assumed I was a hippie?" Sam said, thumbing at his high and tight. "Wow . . . *You* should be the detective, Bernard." He looked at the kid's Reagan button, thought about him getting slapped, thought about him shooting BBs at orphans and contemplated the special terror of being invisible. This kid's only hope of being noticed was to attack everything denied him. No one wanted to party with him, so partying was the enemy. No one wanted to have sex with him, so sex was the enemy. No one felt sorry for him, so compassion was the enemy. His reactionary stance was nothing more than an outcast's sour grapes, his obnoxiousness the only alternative to being utterly ignored. If he hadn't just caught him plinking a ten-year-old in the face, Sam might have felt sorry for the kid.

"Prescription face soap?" Sam said as he headed for the door.

Bernard continued pretending to read. "I would appreciate your not making light of my medical condition."

"What medical condition?"

"I have overly active sebaceous glands."

Sam snorted. "So zits."

In the hallway, Sam heeled Bernard's door shut. He looked around and then took a small leather pouch out of his pocket. He selected one of the picks inside, coaxed open Dale's lock, stepped within and quietly closed the door behind him.

It was not the room of a poor kid. He had a high-end turntable, a giant color Trinitron, a ColecoVision video game console and a Betamax.

Oddly enough, he also had a large canister vacuum cleaner. The room was certainly tidy. Immaculate, in fact. On a recently Lemon Pledged bookshelf, Sam found a yearbook and looked up Dale Lauferson. Skinny, handsome in kind of a sleazy way. Ice-blue eyes and thick, curly brown hair. His interests and activities included nothing. Sam began going through Dale's drawers and desk, kicking through the closet, patting the floor and walls for any loose slats, looking under the bed, under and in the mattress. No book.

Then Sam's eyes fell on a large pyramid of giant chocolate bars carefully stacked on a bookshelf next to a Bible.

The top three bars were, indeed, chocolate. The next ten contained vacuum-sealed bricks of pot carefully covered with gold foil and re-sleeved with the chocolate wrappers. None of them contained a stolen book.

Two, however, contained unmarked videocassettes wrapped in cellophane.

Sam turned on Dale's TV and Betamax and popped in one of the tapes.

The camera panned and tilted until it settled on the painting of the school's founder, Mason Alderhut, over the safe in Ms. Lee's office. Dale entered the frame and deliberately skewed the painting. Then he began dusting.

Sam heard a door open and close. Ms. Lee entered the frame, sat at her desk and pointed at the camera. "What's wrong with it?" she asked.

"I don't know. I took off the hose, but there's no blockage. Maybe a fuse," Dale said.

"Well, it can't be the only one on campus," Ms. Lee said, "and I want this room clean, so talk to Mr. Speck."

"Yes, ma'am," Dale said. He grabbed her wastepaper basket and emptied it into a janitor's bin, which he then trundled away. Sam heard the door open and close again.

After a minute or so, Ms. Lee looked up with a frown and turned her head to see the painting of Alderhut. The sight of it so noticeably off-kilter made her jump slightly. She looked around nervously, then got up, removed the painting and opened the safe. Sam saw the combination clear as day. Ms. Lee did a quick inventory of the books within, then shut and locked the safe. She put the painting back, leveled it and worried her chin with her hand for a bit as she looked about fretfully. Finally, she settled back into her chair and resumed her business.

Sam opened the large canister vacuum cleaner. He saw a Betamovie video camera seated inside it, the lens of the camera lined up with the vacuum hose port.

So Dale had scoped out the combo, then outsourced the burglary to Jimmy. Pros and cons to that for Dale. On the pro side, the dirty work was done by Jimmy, and if he got caught the problem was all his. Dale had a perfect alibi with the faculty party. And if Jimmy said Dale had put him up to it, well, Jimmy's word against anyone else probably didn't carry much weight since he was a stoner and an idiot. And that, of course, was the con side. The problem with needing someone to be stupid enough to steal something for you is that you have to rely on someone who's stupid enough to steal something for you.

Sam popped the second tape into the VCR. It appeared to have been made here in Dale's room and featured him having sex with a pretty brunette. It was clear from the unselfconscious way the girl gave herself to the various acts, to the love in her eyes and to the obvious indifference she had for the frame, that she was unaware of being videotaped. And it was clear from Dale's deliberate positioning and his rather mannered performance that he was very much aware that he was on camera. Sam thought at first that Dale was covered with tattoos that had been hidden by clothes in his yearbook shot. Then he realized they were scars, burn scars, over most of his body. Whatever had happened to this kid, it was a miracle he was still alive. Kind of a wasted miracle, Sam thought, as the kid was shaping up to be a world-class scumbag.

Sam returned to Dale's yearbook and flipped back to his picture. Written next to it was a gushing love note full of inside jokes and signed "Laura." Sam began scanning the yearbook for Lauras and found Dale's costar: Laura Hershlag.

She'd been easy to find. There were pictures of her playing the piano, directing plays, making jewelry, winning debates . . . the activities section was more or less a collage dedicated to her overachievement. Sam ejected the sex tape and pocketed it.

T he second Dale comes back to his room," Sam said, pressing his card to Bernard's forehead, where it stuck, "you call me. You do not tell Dale. You deviate from these instructions, I'll have a little word with the headmaster about your target practice."

"I only hit one of them," Bernard whined.

"You're an angel," Sam said as he grabbed the air rifle and headed out the door.

12

PAUL SPITZ

Paul usually felt like a twenty-watt bulb with a million volts pumped into it. Despite football practices, extra time in the weight room (which he had to sneak into, because he was told he was working out too much) and various other activities he'd pushed to the back of his mind, he could never expel all his energy. He didn't fall asleep easily, but once he did, he was like a denning Kodiak, and just as cheerful as one when roused.

His phone had been ringing for a solid four minutes before he answered it. In his first attempt, he swatted the base right off his dresser. Growling, he pulled himself out of bed, found the handset cord and jerked, flailing himself in the face with the receiver. He roared and punched a hole in the drywall.

"The *fuck* is this!"

"Operations," Harriet said. "We're reporting a malfunction in your radiator."

Paul turned to his radiator and stared at it. "What's wrong with it?"

"That's what I'm trying to find out," Harriet said. "Do you hear it hissing ever?"

"Well . . . yeah," Paul said. "All radiators . . . isn't that what they do?"

"Yes and no," Harriet said. "What kind of hiss does it make?"

"What?"

"What's the hiss sound like? Make it for me."

Paul attempted to make a radiator hiss.

Harriet hummed thoughtfully. "Sounds like what we call a distributing stream double-pipe hiss."

"Is that bad?"

"Usually no, but if the pressure vents along the wrong steam conduit, it could knock out heat to the whole dorm, and since it originated in your room, you could be on the hook for repairs."

"What?"

"And we're probably talking a few grand."

"But I didn't do anything!" Paul said, hastily moving a Motörhead poster over the hole he'd just punched in the wall. He was chagrined to discover that the poster had already been covering a dent he'd made on a previous occasion. He vaguely remembered making it, but not why (though the fact that he'd made it with his forehead helped explain the haziness of his recollection).

"It's part of the agreement your parents or guardian signed when you enrolled here."

"That is bullshit!" Paul said.

"Calm down," Harriet said. "It's probably just a clog. We can have someone there between twelve and two."

"I have football practice," Paul said.

"Can you skip it?" Harriet said. "Shouldn't take more than an hour."

"No, I can't skip practice," Paul replied, barely able to fathom the absurdity of this request.

"I mean, suit yourself, but the next window is Friday, and if it blows before then, it could cost you."

"Can't I just leave my door open?" Paul asked.

"Well . . ." Harriet said, hedging, "we really like someone to be there. Liability."

"Just . . . I can't be here! I'll leave the door unlocked, just come in and fix it!"

Harriet begrudgingly consented and hung up. Later, she watched through binoculars as Paul left for practice. When he was halfway to the field, she made for his room, which, true to his word, he had left unlocked.

Once inside, she was almost staggered by the pungent

teenage boy smell, an acrid mix of sweat, dirt and . . . Well, she didn't really want to think about what else.

Despite the rankness, the room was relatively tidy. Or appeared so, until she opened the closet, in which a wall of filthy clothes was wedged. Paul had rammed the closet door against the mass of dirty laundry with such force, she could see signs of strain at the hinges. He had effectively rendered his closet a trash compactor, which made her doubt he'd put anything of value in it. She might just be telling herself that, she realized, because she gagged at the thought of poking through his underwear. At the very least, she thought, she could save it for last.

What stood out to her was what looked like a low side table next to his desk. It was covered with a toile fabric that looked oddly grandmotherly, especially juxtaposed with the rest of his adolescent decor. On closer inspection, she realized that the cloth was roughly trimmed, as though he'd taken a scissors to someone's drapes, and that it covered a padlocked mini-fridge.

Evidently, Paul did not trust his memory for numbers, because she found the combination scribbled on the back of a picture of Dick Butkus tacked to Paul's corkboard. Inside the mini-fridge were bottles of pills, Dianabol and Anadrol, vials of liquid labeled Deca-Durabolin and Winstrol V and a box of syringes.

On Paul's dresser was a flight of aftershaves and male

colognes. By mixing a few of them together she was able to reproduce what she had smelled in the planetarium the morning of the attack. At the back of his bottom dresser drawer, Harriet found a rubber werewolf mask.

P aul returned from practice more than a little proud of himself. During a scrimmage, he had hit Tony Devito so hard, he'd knocked him out. They couldn't wake him up, and he had to be carried off on a stretcher. Paul wasn't sure what Tony's condition was currently, but it had been a clean hit and totally legal, so even if he was dead, Paul couldn't get in trouble. Now that he thought about it, Paul wasn't totally sure the guy's name was Tony Devito. He was a new defensive end and they hadn't talked much.

Paul's mood soured abruptly when he opened his mini-fridge. It was empty except for a note, which read: "It's no fun being messed with, is it?"

13

LAURA

B lood spurted in an almost comic arc as the girl plunged a bread knife into the boy's chest. He moaned, staggered, fell, and then dissolved into giggles at the eighth thrust. The girl sighed and stared out into the audience.

Laura Hershlag sat in the middle of the auditorium, every seat to herself. She exhaled loudly and jabbed her forehead with her fingers, the eight bracelets on her arm clacking together with disapproval. "Jake?"

"I'm sorry, it tickles," said Jake as Niloofar lifted his shirt and looked at the blood packs, most of which had deployed.

"The blood okay?" Niloofar shouted.

"It's a little . . . Maybe pull it back twenty percent. Nancy, can you try to stab him someplace he isn't ticklish?" asked Laura.

Sam had been watching the rehearsal, rapt, for the last fifteen minutes. The play took place in a Nicaraguan village where a slimy CIA operative was trying to recruit people to the Contras. He gave them illustrated handbooks on how to ice-pick fuel lines, make Molotov cocktails and torture and kill anyone loyal to the Sandinistas. The CIA scumbag, whose name was Dale and who was covered with burns he'd received doing something nefarious in Chile, attempted to rape a sixteen-year-old Nicaraguan girl, who then stabbed him to death. Sam didn't think it was a very good play, but he marveled at the lavishness of the production.

"She's not doing it right," Sam said.

Laura snapped her head around so quickly that one of the four large hoop earrings hanging from her left lobe nearly hit Sam in the nose. Sam nudged his chin in Nancy's direction. "She needs to keep the blade horizontal if it's supposed to slip through his ribs, which it would need to, a knife that size, a girl her size, to cause the kind of blood you're showing. More believable would be if she hit an artery in the neck."

"Who are you?" Laura asked.

"My name's Sam Gregory. You Laura Hershlag?"

Laura took in Sam's buzz cut and build. "Oh, God, what are you, like, some sort of asshole from the government here to shut us down?"

Sam looked at her, baffled. "You think the government's worried about a high school play?"

"Laura?" said Jake, eyeing Sam nervously.

"I can handle this," Laura said, not taking her eyes off Sam. "You don't scare me. When people find out about all the torture and killing and other illegal crap Reagan's been funding in Central America, he's going to get impeached."

Sam shrugged. "Doesn't sound like the kind of thing a president gets impeached for, but I'm not here about your play. I'm here about your video."

Laura's eyes flashed. "What?"

Sam held up the videotape. Laura looked as if she'd lost all of the blood being mopped up onstage.

"Any chance you can cut rehearsal short?" Sam asked.

Laura did, then quickly gathered her things and speed-walked to her room. Sam followed her in silence. She stood nervously in her doorway windmilling her arm for him to hustle inside, the bangles hula-hooping about her wrist. Sam entered and she quickly shut the door after him.

Laura folded her arms and stared at him for a few moments, fuming. Her eyes flicked to the videotape. "What is that?" she said.

"It's a bootleg of *The Muppet Movie*," Sam said. "What do you think it is?"

"Why do you have it and what do you want?" she said.

"I have it because I'm looking for a kid named Dale

Lauferson," Sam said. "He was not in his room. This was." He tossed her the tape and she caught it. "How'd you find out he made that?"

Laura fished a hammer out of her drawer. "Dale told me. The other night."

Sam watched her smash open the casing and spool loose its innards. He scratched the back of his neck. "Listen . . . I'm a little uncomfortable asking this, but I guess I have to. You didn't kill him, did you?"

Laura looked as though Sam had just announced that he was pregnant. "No."

He shrugged. "I mean, if anyone had it coming—"

"Just . . . What do you want?" she asked.

"I want to know where he is."

Laura grabbed a scissors and began cutting through the handfuls of tape over a wastepaper basket. "No idea. And though I didn't kill him, I honestly don't care if he's dead."

Sam nodded at the tape. "May I assume that Dale wasn't driven to tell you about that by a pang of conscience?"

She grunted and struck a match. "You may." She dropped the match in the wastepaper basket.

"So what did he want?"

Laura gripped her left arm and looked around the room. "Help with this paper we have to write," she said.

"Really?" said Sam, fascinated. "On what?"

"*Paradise Lost*," Laura said. "It's this poem by Milton about the fall of—"

"So Dale," Sam interrupted, "the campus drug dealer, was so worried about the grade he was going to get on his English paper that he decided to blackmail you for help on it with this sex tape?"

She shrugged and cleared her throat. "He's a weird guy."

"A few days after getting his idiot friend to steal a rare book for him," Sam said, "Dale shows up and tries to blackmail you into doing something for him. It wasn't his homework. Are you hiding the book for him?"

"No."

"Your dad some rare book collector willing to buy it off him on the sly?"

"No."

"Well, what the hell did Dale want?"

"A necklace, all right?"

Sam blinked at her, confused. "Huh?"

"I make jewelry," she said. "Dale made me make a necklace for him."

"What kind of necklace?" Sam asked.

"I don't know! It was something he found in that stupid book he stole, okay?" She began rooting through her drawers.

"What?" Sam asked.

"The book has instructions on how to make this necklace. He sure wasn't into any of that witchy stuff when we were dating."

"Witchy stuff?"

"Whatever it is. I mean, he said some weird spell over it while I was making it."

"*Spell?*"

"That's what it sounded like."

"And you have no idea why he's doing this?"

"Don't know, don't care." Finally, in one of the drawers, she found a clay mold for the necklace, which she handed to Sam. "Here's the mold I made for it. I don't know or have anything else. I swear. Can you please leave me alone now?"

Sam pocketed the mold and turned to go.

"I'd appreciate you not telling anyone about this," she said.

"It's already forgotten," Sam said. "And don't be so embarrassed. Not like you're the first girl who's slept with a loser to get back at her dad."

Laura straightened and folded her arms across her chest. "I did not have sex with Dale to get back at my father."

Sam shrugged and lit a Kent. "I'm just saying I've done a lot worse. When I wanted to rebel against my dad, I went to war. It's not like you killed anybody." With that, he was gone.

14

OFF THE RECORD

Paul stared at the door to the mini-fridge, which remained clutched in his hand. The rest of the fridge lay near the bathroom, its rear coils having dug long scratches in the floor after his abrupt yanking loosed it from its hinges and sent it skidding.

Paul had worked very hard to make himself what he was. Less than five years ago, you would have described him as downright sickly.

"Look at this kid," his old man would say while Paul struggled to carry in bags of groceries or wheel garbage bins to the curb. "A light breeze'd blow him over. Are you sure he's mine, Steph?" Paul's mother would swirl her wine and put the least effort possible into a smile.

Paul's dad was all man. Six foot three, 210 pounds, and bold as a peacock. A long mane of chestnut hair, a mustache and muttonchops, busy Christian Dior shirts open to the navel showing off his tan, gold chains and chest hair. Every place he strutted into, he was always one stare away from "What are you looking at?" and two from "Let's take it outside."

And he kept fit. Jogging, platform tennis, weight lifting. No middle-age spread for Paul's dad. Sometimes he'd let Paul hold his feet while he did sit-ups. Paul could smell the Dentyne his dad chewed constantly when he'd exhale in measured bursts while crunching his elbows to the opposite knees.

One night, his mother sent Paul to the twenty-four-hour pharmacy to pick up one of her many prescriptions. He was on his way home when he realized he could take ten minutes off his trip if he cut through Bera Park. All the kids were told to avoid Bera Park after sundown, but he was in a mood to prove his manhood. He would not be scared of this dark, deserted park or its whispered dangers. He ignored the creak of the rusted merry-go-round and the rasp of windblown leaves as they skittered across his path.

He assumed, at first, that the rustling of the bushes off to his left was just the wind or squirrels. But then he heard distinctly human grunting and swearing. He stared in horror as two men emerged from the bushes, quickly shoving their shirttails back into their pants and zipping up. The men caught sight of Paul. Paul recognized one of them but pretended he hadn't, turned and marched out of the park at a heady clip.

A block from the park, Paul felt a hand on his shoulder. "You know that's . . . The park's not really a safe place for kids after dark," his dad said.

Paul stared at his shoes as they walked home. He memorized every inch of his Pumas—the stitching, the scuffs, the logo—as his dad explained how, crazy thing, he'd come across that guy getting mugged. Paul's dad had fought off the attackers, but as they ran away—the cowards—they chucked the wedding ring, watch and wallet they'd just grabbed from that poor bastard into the bushes. Paul's dad was just helping that guy find his lost valuables when Paul happened by.

Paul's dad started traveling a lot after that. For work. The subject of his dad came up one day at recess during dodgeball. Jeannie Wyshak smirked at Paul, extended her arm and let her hand droop limply. Paul grabbed the ball out of Jim Mikolowski's hand, ran up to her and whaled her in the face with it, point-blank, breaking her glasses. He pulled two weeks of detention and the threat of suspension but refused to tell the vice principal what had provoked the assault. He just silently cleaned blackboard erasers.

Jeannie's three older brothers caught up to Paul one day as he was walking home and beat the crap out of him, leaving him on the Murdochs' lawn with their spit on his face. That was okay. He'd gotten in a few good licks. In fact, he'd nearly bitten off Chip Wyshak's earlobe. And he hadn't minded getting hit. Honestly, he'd kind of liked it.

Two weeks later, Paul hit Adam Carr with a tackle that knocked his retainer out. Adam Carr was the biggest kid in Paul's seventh-grade class and twice Paul's size. This was during a flag football game and deemed unnecessarily rough, so Paul was kicked off the field. But Coach Douglas had clocked the tackle. He planted a foot on the bench where Paul had been sent to sit out the rest of PE.

"You like hitting people," Coach Douglas said. It wasn't a question, so Paul didn't reply. The coach stared at Paul for a moment, and Paul looked at his reflection in the coach's mirrored aviators. Paul didn't like his reflection. Somehow, he always looked smaller than he expected.

Coach Douglas took a clipboard out of his gym bag and filled out a form. "Take this to the equipment room after school." He ripped out the form and handed it to Paul. "See you at practice."

His first game, Paul sacked the QB twice. After that, football was his world. It was all he wanted to do. He organized his routine around it. Breakfast, morning practice, school, afternoon practice, dinner, carry his mom, usually passed out next to an empty bottle of Chablis by that point, up to her bedroom, watch football if it was Monday night or read about it if it wasn't, sleep, dream about football, repeat.

Paul considered his mother a familiar presence, but he had not relied on her for anything in some time. So he was a little baffled when everyone started expressing concern over leaving him "unattended" when they finally packed her off someplace to dry out.

His dad called to say that he was just too busy with work to drop everything and move back in, but Paul's grandparents on his mom's side were loaded and willing to pay Paul's way at Danforth Putnam. That would be his new home.

He signed up for football before unpacking his bags. But he soon realized that this was a level up from the Pee Wee league he was used to. His 148 pounds were not going to cut it. By consuming massive amounts of roast beef and peanut butter, and spending every spare moment working out, he got himself to 177. That made him big enough for a high school linebacker, but barring a major growth spurt, which no one thought likely, he was not going to get recruited for college football. And he could forget about pro.

Dale was mopping the dining hall early one morning when Paul came in for breakfast. Dale watched Paul crack six eggs into a glass of orange juice and down it.

"Can I get you a cup of coffee with some bacon in it?" Dale asked. Paul gave him a warning look. Dale laughed. He rested the mop against a wall and sat opposite Paul. "What do you bench?" Dale asked.

"More than you," Paul said.

"No doubt," said Dale. "I was just reading that every member of the Steelers offensive line can bench over five hundred pounds. Can you believe that?"

Paul looked around. Aside from the line cooks, who didn't really have a good view of them, he and Dale were alone in the dining hall. If he knocked Dale's teeth out, he could probably claim Dale started it.

"Twenty years ago," Dale continued, "do you know how many Steelers could bench over five hundred pounds? None."

"What's your point?" Paul asked.

Dale looked around and leaned in with a smile. "My point is . . . I know their secret."

Paul's max bench press was 180. Less than a month later, he was benching sets of 225 without warming up. There was no going back after that. He never even considered it. There was a cost, sure. The rages, the blackouts, the errands Dale made him do in trade when he was short on cash. But it was his life.

Staring at that empty mini-fridge, he felt like a deep-sea diver noticing that his air hose had been cut.

His phone rang.

"Get my note?" Harriet said.

"I'm going to kill you," Paul hissed. "I'm going to tear your intestines out and force you to eat them."

"Sounds like I've caught you at a bad time," Harriet said. "I'll call back."

She hung up. Paul waffled the mini-fridge's door with punches.

His phone rang again.

"I am going to rip your head off and shit down your throat," Paul said.

"Like you shit down Josh Beckman's sousaphone?"

"That wasn't me, it was McCain!" Paul said indignantly.

He sounded oddly huffy to Harriet for a guy who'd just threatened to shit down her throat. "How did you get the steroids?"

"None of your business!" Paul said.

Harriet flushed a toilet.

"What are you doing?" Paul asked, panicked.

"Flushing some of your pills. I don't want to clog the john, so I'll just do a small handful every time you don't answer me."

"Stop! I need those!"

Harriet laughed. "I looked up the medical uses for those drugs in the library. Do you suffer from pituitary-deficient dwarfism or postmenopausal osteoporosis?"

"What do you want?"

"Where are you getting the steroids?"

"What the hell do you care?"

She flushed again.

"I . . . Dale Lauferson. What is the big deal? They're not illegal!"

"Prescription drugs you don't have a prescription for? I bet you'd get kicked off the team at least, if not out of the school. Did I mention I'm recording this call?"

Paul started to see spots. "You . . . This means . . . I don't even know what you're talking . . . And you just admitted to stealing my property! You broke the law!" he said, impressing himself with this legal maneuvering.

"I haven't stolen anything," Harriet said. "Check your laundry." She hung up.

Paul tore through the dirty clothes in his closet. Eventually he realized that she had separated out the pills and vials, tied them in clean socks and lobbed them behind his wall of unwashed things. It took him hours to fully sort out his stash.

The voice. He knew that voice. Where did he know her voice from?

He was returning the clean socks in which Harriet had divided his steroids to his dresser when he saw the werewolf mask. He stared at it numbly for a good fifteen seconds, his brain synapses sluggishly making connections. It was that little Black girl with the giant glasses. The one who'd spazzed out when they razzed her nerd club. This was payback for that. What the hell was her name? Well . . . she'd be easy enough to find.

15

FLYNN

Flynn, a stout, windburned guy with tufts of gray chest hair peeking out over a cable-knit sweater older than Sam, scraped the hull of a sailboat that was suspended by a winch inside the boathouse. In several slips were motorboats so clean their chrome was almost blinding. The same was true of Flynn's gold incisor when his lips curled back and he treated Sam to a fragrant guffaw.

"Think I'd know if a boat was taken," Flynn said, hefting one of the heavy padlocked chains mooring the boats. "Nope, they chained up good."

"Any other way this Dale kid might have gotten off the island?" Sam asked.

"Maybe he flew," Flynn offered.

"You guys have planes?"

"Nah, I mean, maybe he flapped his arms and took off," Flynn said. For a good five seconds the two men just looked at each other. "It was a joke," Flynn finally explained.

"Ah. Good one," Sam said. "Maybe he made a raft?"

"Who is this kid, Robinson Crusoe?" said Flynn. "Besides, in this current, a raft wouldn't make it past that breakwater. And I don't see any gulls peckin' at what's left of him, so I guess he didn't try."

"No one's seen Dale anywhere since yesterday," Sam said. "You're sure there's no way he could have gotten to the mainland?"

"All the boats are present and accounted for." Flynn gave a mock salute. "And the ferry doesn't come again till Friday. So, unless this kid knows magic . . ."

He went quiet. He nodded at the pack of Kents in Sam's pocket. "I'll take one of those."

Sam shook a Kent out of the pack for Flynn and lit it.

"Thanks." Flynn nodded at Sam's tattoo. "You in Nam?"

"Uh-huh. You a marine?"

"Navy. Korea. Saw some shit there."

"I bet."

"Not just combat. There was this island. There's like a few thousand of them off the Korean coast. Fishing village. Nobody wanted to talk to us. Some shaman warned them not to. But we had food and medicine, so they did. Next day, we're on the boat and we see a ten-foot tiger go into the village. Now, tigers are big in Korean culture, but even back then no one had seen one in a while. Definitely not on an island. Well, we raised all kinds of Cain, trying to warn the villagers, and we tried to shoot the thing, but our bullets just bounced off it. It ate every one of them. Bones and all. Then it turned into a woman. She laughed at us and sent a wave that nearly capsized the ship. Then she turned into smoke. And disappeared."

Sam nodded. "In Saigon, I saw a hooker beat three GIs in a row at pool, holding the cue between her legs and . . . Yeah, no, your story's better."

He noticed a few spearguns mounted on the wall. "What are the harpoons for?"

Flynn stared at Sam without blinking. "In case."

"In case what?" The tips of the harpoons appeared, at first, to have foil wrapped around them. When Sam looked more closely, he realized they'd been plated with what appeared to be silver.

Flynn nodded slowly, certainly. "I'm just ready. Whatever comes at me." He gave Sam a wink, which said, "We understand each other." They didn't.

"'Kay . . . well . . . thanks for your time," Sam said and happily took his leave of Flynn.

As he headed away from the dock, Sam passed a twelve-foot statue of the school's founder, Mason Alderhut. Chiseled into the statue was the same smug grin Sam had noticed in the painting in Ms. Lee's office. There was something about his smile that Sam found incredibly unnerving. It wasn't a pleasant smile, certainly. It had no trace of warmth or good-will. And it betrayed a deeply sinister amusement. Though that was the eyes, more than the mouth. Sam had seen eyes like that before. A corporal in his company had walked up to a Vietnamese kid one day and calmly set his dog on fire. While the kid screamed and chased after the dog and tried to put out the fire, the corporal had just stood there smiling and quietly pissing himself. When they tightened the last strap of his straitjacket and packed him into a chopper, he was still quietly smiling, his eyes the same as Mason Alderhut's, wet and electric.

Sam stood for a long while in the massive shadow of Mason Alderhut, trapped by those horrible eyes. He was about to tear himself away when he noticed that peeking out from beneath Mason Alderhut's marble cloak was part of a necklace. It appeared identical to the mold Laura had given him.

16

THE SUPPLIER

Harriet stared at Dale Lauferson's yearbook picture for a full two minutes. She could not place him anywhere. Fortunately, her friend Niloofar could.

Niloofar was not in the drama clique, per se; she was a member of the tech crew. While the drama kids practiced their scenes, mirror exercises and animal walks and gave each other back rubs, compared leg warmers, stretched, vocalized and cattily bemoaned the plight of Broadway ("Another *West Side Story* revival at the Minskoff. How fresh."), she padded around them, painting scenery, building sets and hanging lights. They never seemed to notice her. They would tell one another about their sexual infidelities, take their clothes completely off during costume changes, make out, have nervous

breakdowns ("What if I'm just too character to ever get leading man roles?") and not even slow down or lower their voices
when she clanged past hoisting Fresnels.

She didn't resent this, really. It just puzzled her. She
supposed it was simply the nature of actors to be completely
unselfconscious (or self-centered, if you wanted to take it personally). At any rate, she sometimes felt like a xenoanthro-
pologist from the Starship *Enterprise*, sent to observe an alien
culture but not interact with it.

At seventeen, Laura Hershlag was the grande dame of the
Danforth Putnam drama circle. She held them all in an almost cultlike thrall, having evolved from performer to writer/
director/producer. She was always mounting some incredibly
earnest play, which meant she had parts to offer, which meant
that the rest of these attention-starved exhibitionists would
nod along, rapt, while Laura held forth about Artaud's The-
atre of Cruelty or something called *Verfremdungseffekt*.

Dale, like Niloofar, was not in the drama clique. He was,
however, Laura's ex. Niloofar had seen Dale canoodling with
Laura in the wings during a performance of her book of
Genesis–inspired one-act *Eden: Rape Scene*. Apparently, the
affair was now over and, according to the chatter among
Laura's troupe, had ended badly.

Harriet was enormously grateful for this point of entry.
She'd thought about looking up Dale's room number in the
student exchange, staking him out and confronting him, but

to what end? She had no power to make him talk. And it seemed unlikely that he'd believe she was a prospective buyer.

But an aggrieved ex-girlfriend? That was gold. Laura was likely to have inside information and be motivated to spill it.

Harriet's reception at the drama department was frosty. One of the actors recalled—seemed, frankly, to have memorized—an unfavorable review she'd written ("The spring musical *Mame* should be spelled as *Maim* in order to accurately convey what Shonda Dworsky does to 'Gooch's Song'").

Eventually, one of the thespians begrudgingly helped her. He was nursing a thermos full of what smelled like honey and lemon tea and had the largest scarf Harriet had ever seen coiled up to his nose. He wouldn't speak, he explained in a written note, because he was protecting "his instrument" for a number of challenging solos in the Glee Club's Autumn Jam, but he believed Laura was practicing the piano in the basement of the old music building. He asked that Harriet remember this kindness if she found herself reviewing his performance (adding that he agreed that Shonda's rendition of "Gooch's Song" had been a little pitchy).

17

THE PRACTICE ROOM

What the hell do you know, you piece of shit, Laura thought. She'd been fuming since her encounter with Sam and marched down the steps into the basement of the old music building, sheet music clutched in her fist like a warrant she was about to slap in someone's face. She kicked open the heavy metal double doors to the lower corridor and let them slam behind her as she barreled through. Invade my privacy, throw it in my face and then act like you *know* me? You're a scumbag with a sex tape, you filth! You know nothing! You *are* nothing!

She was not a patient person under any circumstances and Sam had worked her into a lather, so it was a particularly bad time for her to open the practice room she had reserved and find Bernard squinting at some ancient sheet music, his lips wrapped around some bizarre black woodwind instrument.

"Do you mind?" he asked without looking up. "I'm trying to practice the krummhorn."

"What?"

Bernard gave an exasperated sigh, then slowly and deliberately said, "The. Krumm. Horn. The double-reeded fifteenth-century instrument?" He rolled his eyes at her ignorance.

"I have this room reserved, Bernard."

"Uh . . . you *had* this room reserved," Bernard corrected. "You were a no-show, so the room goes to whoever is waiting and that was I."

"What do you mean 'no-show'? I'm right here."

"Now, maybe, but the room was reserved for"—he swung his arm in an exaggerated arc and examined his watch—"three minutes ago, GMT. You didn't arrive by the designated time, ergo, the room is mine."

"Every other practice room on this floor is empty," Laura said. "Why do you have to use this one?"

"It has the best acoustics," Bernard said, picking up his krummhorn and braying into it.

"It has the best piano, which you're not even using."

"Tell it to the krummhorn, sister," Bernard said, then returned to his plangent honking.

Laura slowly licked her teeth with her tongue, then took a deep breath and smiled.

"You sure I'm late?"

Bernard laughed and tapped his watch. "Uh, yeah. This is only a Swiss watch? From Switzerland? Which they're only incredibly famous for?"

"No way. Let me see."

Bernard extended his wrist. She held it, grabbed a heavy wooden metronome off the piano and shattered the face of his watch with it.

"I don't know," Laura said, frowning at his watch. "I think it might be losing time."

"What the hell is wrong with you!" Bernard shrieked. "My grandfather gave me that!"

"The krummhorn's next, shithead," she said, hefting the metronome.

"Don't you even *think* about touching my krummhorn," he said, hugging it protectively.

"No one ever thinks about touching your krummhorn, Bernard."

"Okay, you're disgusting. All your friends are disgusting. Everything about you and everyone you know makes me sick and—"

"Bernard. Several grave infractions have been committed here. Can you really afford to waste precious seconds not alerting the authorities? You're letting society down."

"You do not know with whom you're messing," Bernard

hissed, grabbing his music and his krummhorn and stomping out. "You do *not* know! Bi . . . bitch!"

"Yeah, so long, sheriff," Laura said, then lazily swung the door shut after him.

Laura uncreased her music, took a few calming breaths and started to play. Her fingers faltered, and that only increased her anger at Sam's parting shot. You think I slept with Dale to get back at my dad? Shows what you know.

She had slept with Dale to get back at her mom. Her mom, who had audibly apologized to everyone in her row every time Laura, her seven-year-old daughter, made a mistake during her first piano recital; her mom, who started "forgetting" to pick her up from school when she heard one of the other kids call her chubby so that she'd have to walk the three miles home; her mom, who told her to "laugh off" the passes the drama teacher made at her when she was thirteen until after she was cast as the lead in her middle school's production of *Oklahoma*; her mom, who pitted her accomplishments against those of every other child in the world and who deducted affection for every nonperfect score, nonperfect performance, nonperfect game—

Laura hit another wrong note and began pounding the keys with her fists. She picked up the metronome and threw it across the room with a battle cry. She grabbed her sheet music, tore it into tiny pieces, threw them into the air, then batted the pieces to the ground and stomped on them. She sat at the piano again and rested her head on her arms, panting.

Dale. The first time she'd noticed him, a couple of lacrosse players were throwing plastic cups at him while he was busing trays in the cafeteria. He looked as though he didn't even notice the cups bouncing off him. A week later, an anonymous tip caused security guards to do a random search and they found pot in the lockers of those lacrosse players. The lacrosse players were given a chance to atone, to attend meetings and to lead authorities to the source of the weed, but they swore up and down that they'd never seen the drugs before, they didn't take them and didn't know where they'd come from, so they were expelled.

The next time Laura noticed Dale, he was cheating off her math test. He saw her watching him and just smiled at her.

"I could have busted you for that," she said after class.

"Yeah, thanks," he said, then kissed her full on the mouth. She looked around in shock, wondering if anyone else had witnessed this startling embrace, but they were alone in the hallway.

He winked at her. "I got to go clean some toilets," he said and sauntered off, striking a match against a locker and lighting a joint. In the middle of the hall! He was gone before Mr. Logue emerged from his office, snuffling with alarm. "Who was smoking?" he asked her. She shrugged.

She remembered the first time she saw Dale naked, those

horrible scars coiled about him from ankle to neck, lapping at his face but leaving it untouched. He had not prepared her and stood staring at her with his ice-blue eyes, daring her to be repulsed. She was not. His scars only made him more exotic, even mythical, like some ifrit, a creature of sex and danger made flesh from flame.

One of the best days of Laura's life had been when she'd taken Dale, unannounced, to the beach club. Her mother had noisily rattled her iced tea while Dale talked about a fingernail infection he'd gotten from cleaning bathrooms. And when Dale had taken off his shirt—oh, when he had taken off his shirt! Laura had kept her eyes locked on her mother's face, drinking in her change in color from peach to light green to a mottled blush, her lower lip disappearing and her eyes bulging with aneurysmal intensity as Dale's scars were displayed for all to see.

The way she had looked at her mother that day, she realized, her heart twisting, was just how Dale had looked at her when he'd showed her the sex tape. He'd taken the same hateful satisfaction in her shocking exposure that she had in his. She could not fathom what she had done to warrant this hate. She had been the wronged party when they broke up. On the night he showed up at her dorm with that videotape she'd half assumed he'd come slithering in for a long-overdue apology. But he had not apologized—he was probably, she guessed, incapable of remorse, something she had not realized until she stared into his smiling, awful, spiteful eyes that night. She had never been more than a thing to Dale. No one in the world was more than a thing to Dale.

Laura rested her left cheek on the piano keys with a discordant thrum and let out a mighty sigh. She stared at her right hand and began walking it through a blues progression. She wondered why she was right-handed. Rather, she wondered why people had, for the most part, a dominant half. Why was it so rare for even the sides of someone's own body to share power? It was depressing to realize that life was so inherently agonistic that it even pitted one half of yourself against the other half and declared a winner.

The lights overhead began to flicker. She stopped playing and glared at the lights for a long moment, daring them to continue being just one more thing to test her patience today. The lights stopped flickering and she felt unreasonably glad at having won the stare-down.

Moments after she resumed playing, however, the lights flickered again and then died. She squeezed her eyes shut and pounded the keys with her forehead. "Unbelievable," she whispered.

Something drifted by in the corridor outside her room, just a dark sliver of it visible through the small window in the practice room door. "Bernard?" Laura said. No answer. She stood and opened the door. The hallway was empty.

She could call maintenance about the burned-out light, but that would take forever and eat through all her practice time. Fortunately, the supply closet was unlocked, so she gathered a few light bulbs and a stepladder and returned to the practice room. She could get in trouble for this. Yep, you're a real rebel, she thought as she screwed in a new bulb, then smiled, then remembered breaking Bernard's watch, then laughed, then remembered the sex tape and cried. She slapped herself in the face and finished screwing in the bulbs.

The lights blazed to life and she glanced away, momentarily blinded. It looked . . . it looked for a second as though something was in the room with her, but when she blinked away the spots and looked again, the room was empty. She took the stepladder back to the supply closet and returned to the practice room. She caught a very strange scent. Electric, mixed with matchstick heads and smoke. The vents probably needed cleaning, she thought, and sat down again to play.

The piano produced no sound. She stood, opened the lid and stared into a mass of snapped strings. It looked as though a lion had clawed through them.

Unhampered by this, the piano began to play itself. Laura screamed and dropped the lid. As it crashed back into place, every light in the basement went out. The piano continued to play, careening exuberantly from the Paganini études to "Sweet Home Chicago" to "In-A-Gadda-Da-Vida."

Laura slapped both hands over her mouth to muffle a shriek as tears streamed down her face. She took her keys out of her pocket and threaded them through the fingers of her right hand, then made a fist. Around her left, she wrapped a heavy metal bracelet. She felt her way to the door and opened it.

She kept her back to the wall and scuttled as fast as she could toward the double doors leading to the stairs. About twenty feet down the hall, she gave in to the impulse to run and bolted down the corridor heedless of the dark. She tripped and sprawled headlong, her ankle wrenched, her keys skittering out of her grip, the parquet floor knocking the breath out of her.

She began to shake in a way that she could not control. She felt close to fainting. She dragged herself down the rest of the corridor, found the double doors and pushed through them.

She scrabbled, hands and feet up the steps, and burst into the woods surrounding the old music building. She filled her lungs with air and was about to scream when she heard a sharp whipping sound. The cry left her noiselessly. She tried to draw breath again but found she could not. She heard a delicate tinkling sound, like a wineglass being tapped before a wedding toast. She looked down and saw the beads of one of her necklaces chinking to the ground, each one speckled with crimson. There was something warm and wet pooling over her chest. She teetered and the rest of her necklaces spooled to the ground. A flapping sound filled her ears. She turned, her vision blurring, and sank to her knees. She stared at death, whose wings folded about her, and she disappeared into its horrible embrace.

18

THE OLD MUSIC BUILDING

The old music building (rarely used since the completion of the new music building) was one of the most remote buildings on campus. It was at the island's eastern edge on a bluff overlooking a rocky coast. The practice rooms were in the basement, accessible through a wide cement staircase on the woodsy side of the building.

As Harriet approached this staircase, something crunched underfoot. She looked down and saw a bead. Then another. They were sprinkled everywhere. Nearby were what looked like strands of silver and gold. The path beneath them was stained red.

She heard a warning hiss. Sprinklers deployed and she jumped back to avoid the spray. She watched the red wash away, watched the gold and silver strands rise in the pooling water and slither off into the high grass.

Harriet darted past the sprinklers and down the steps.

All the lights were out. She found a bank of switches and flicked them on, but to no effect.

Fortunately, since the planetarium blackout, she had begun carrying a small flashlight with her. She thumbed it on and swept the hallway. Something glinted on the floor. She stooped and retrieved a set of keys.

"Hello!" Harriet shouted. "Anyone down here?"

She heard a creak and moved her flashlight to catch a door opening. She smelled something unpleasant, like an industrial floor cleaner but more floral, like a carwash air freshener or . . . wait . . . aftershave.

She heard breathing and whipped her flashlight around to catch a by now familiar werewolf mask. Paul grabbed her by the throat. Her flashlight clattered to the floor as she clawed at his wrist. The toes of her sneakers batted the floor as he lifted her.

"In answer to your note," Paul said, "no. It is no fun being messed with."

Harriet went slack. Paul cocked his head at her, wondering if he'd snapped her neck. He let her go and she punched him as hard as she could in the groin. He doubled over and she ran for the exit.

She'd made it to the top of the steps when he caught her.

He picked her up and carried her to the bluff. She squirmed, but he had her hands pinned so hard behind her, she thought her shoulders would separate. She heard the waves and strained to see them lathering the rocks a hundred feet below.

"Teen suicide is on the rise," Paul said. "I get it. The pressure on us overachievers is a bitch." He raised her over his head. She screamed, flailed, tried to bite anything within reach. He reared back, then jerked suddenly and fell to his knees. She tumbled out of his grasp and crawled away.

She turned and saw someone standing over Paul. It was a man, maybe in his thirties, with a military buzz cut, in a long open coat and sunglasses. He was a big guy, but he looked almost underfed next to Paul's cartoonish bulk. Paul wheezed and coughed into his Halloween mask.

"I get that it's upsetting when you're trick-or-treating and people don't give you candy," Sam told Paul, "but you could have just TPed her house."

Paul charged at Sam, who spun like a matador and sent Paul into an elm. Paul's skull collided with the trunk so forcefully, the poor tree thrummed and lost half its leaves.

Paul shook off the blow as though he'd been hit with a loaf of bread. He turned to Sam with a roar and was about to charge again when the sight of Sam's gun brought him up short.

"That's enough, slim," Sam said. "Let's the three of us go have a chat with the headmaster."

That idea didn't sit well with Paul. He turned and sprinted

into the woods at a speed Sam couldn't quite believe and was not in the least tempted to match.

"You okay?" Sam asked Harriet.

"He tried to kill me," she said.

"Sure looked that way," he said.

"So why the hell didn't you shoot him?" Harriet asked.

Sam gaped at her, then smiled. "You might be the first kid here I can relate to."

W ho are you?" Harriet asked as they walked to the infirmary.

"My name's Sam Gregory. What's your beef with Lon Chaney Jr.?"

"Who?"

"Oh, right. I'm old. The kid in the werewolf mask."

"I found out he's been using steroids."

"Don't see that surprising many people. Guy looks like Stan Lee drew him."

"Are you a new teacher? Why are you here?"

Sam told her he was an insurance company detective and asked if she'd heard about the stolen book. She told him she hadn't.

"You know a kid named Dale Lauferson?" he asked.

Harriet stopped abruptly and stared at him. "Are you messing with me?"

Sam assured her he was not. She asked what Dale had to do with the stolen book. Sam told her.

"Well, according to the caveman you didn't shoot, Dale's also selling steroids," Harriet said.

Sam asked if Harriet had any leads on Dale's whereabouts.

"Didn't know he was missing," Harriet said. "I was just looking for his ex, Laura Hershlag. She might know where he is."

"She doesn't," Sam confided. He relayed his exchange with Laura, omitting any mention of the sex tape.

"He's into witchcraft?" Harriet asked.

"So says his ex. You know any other kids who are into that sort of thing?"

Harriet snorted. "No. I mean, my mom thought *I* was, after reading some hysterical article about D&D."

"What's D&D?"

"Oh right," she said. "You're old." Harriet explained, going on at length about Gary Gygax, which Sam could not believe was a real name.

She was shaking, so Sam wrapped her in his coat. It was twice her size and dragged through the mud and grass behind her like a strange black wedding train.

"So how'd you find out about the steroids?" he asked.

Harriet explained what had befallen the D&D club and how her investigation had led her to Paul.

"You snuck into *that* guy's room?" Sam said. He whistled. "You got some balls."

"I don't," she said, "and I reject the implication that testicles and courage are somehow related."

"Point conceded," Sam said. "Toss me the smokes and the Zippo from the left pocket, would you?"

She clucked disapprovingly but fished the Kents and lighter out of his coat for him anyway. "You're aware, I hope, of the harm you're doing yourself with nicotine, let alone carbon monoxide, arsenic, hydrogen cyanide, benzene and the dozens of other toxic chemicals in cigarettes, and that smoking is responsible for about eighty percent of lung cancer?"

Sam shrugged and cupped his cigarette against the wind as he lit it. "You're pretty risk-averse for someone who just picked a fight with a human rhino."

"*He* picked the fight with *me*," Harriet said. "More important, he fucked with my friends. Do you let people fuck with your friends, Mr. Gregory? Pardon my language."

"Just catch me if I faint," he said. "And . . ."

Sam wondered about that. *Did* he let people fuck with his friends?

He hadn't joined the marines because someone fucked with his friends. Or because he'd thought his country was at risk or because the idea of communism engulfing Asia kept him up at night. He'd joined because Lieutenant Morgenstern, a marine recruiter, talked at a school assembly one day and convinced him that being a marine was as close as anyone could get to being a comic-book superhero. It was a month before graduation, and college was not in Sam's cards, so he picked being in the Justice League over working at his dad's shop. His dad still wouldn't speak to him.

It turned out not to be quite as much fun as Lieutenant Morgenstern had made it seem. And Sam quickly lost a handle on why exactly he was killing people.

That was hard to face. He did not want to be reminded of what he'd chosen and what that had made him, so he avoided contact with anyone he knew before and during the war. And it was probably why he kept people at arm's length now. He really only talked to people for work, and trying to catch someone at insurance fraud didn't usually get you on a Christmas card list. So, though he would like to tell Harriet that no, he didn't let people fuck with his friends, the truth was that he had no friends to be fucked with.

He was surprised to find himself deeply envying Harriet and her righteous sense of purpose. It clearly sustained her in ways he could barely fathom. Here she was, this tiny person, marching through the woods in a giant coat, minutes after someone had tried to fling her off a cliff, ready to take on more because someone had fucked with her friends. She was fueled by a divine spark. Sam wanted one. But, for the life of him, he did not know how in hell he was ever going to come by it.

"How much do you know about your school's founder, Mason Alderhut?" Sam asked.

Harriet shrugged. "Not . . . I mean, nothing, really."

Sam told her about the necklace carved into Alderhut's statue.

"You think our founder was a witch?" she asked.

"I'm not saying he was a witch. Just that he was wearing something . . . witchy. Which is curious, isn't it?"

Harriet agreed that it was. She wanted to know more, but they had arrived at the infirmary and Sam was eager for her to tell that hot doctor what a hero he'd been.

19

MASON ALDERHUT

Dr. O'Megaly examined Harriet and was relieved to find no significant injury.

"Good thing you were there," Dr. O'Megaly told Sam.

He shrugged modestly. "I'm a giver."

A ruddy-faced campus cop with a drinker's paunch and a push-broom mustache took Harriet's statement. He promised her they'd bring Paul in the second they spotted him.

"Grab one of those tranquilizer rifles they use on zoo animals who need dental work," Sam said.

The campus cop chuckled. "I think we can handle one teenager, son."

Sam had a vision of the campus cop in a full body cast. Sam smiled and saluted him.

Sam headed to the library, where Ms. Lee seemed surprised, but not displeased, when Sam asked for a few books on Mason Alderhut. Alderhut appeared to be some sort of personal hero for Ms. Lee and she was delighted, or as close to that as she was capable, to share his accomplishments with Sam. Sam sat on the edge of a high-back leather chair thumbing through the five tomes she'd spread out on the table before him.

Accounts of Mason Alderhut's beginnings varied. Sometimes he was raised in a colony of Marian exiles in the Netherlands before coming to America. Sometimes he was a child of the Earl of Devon, whose wealth and position he disavowed while attending Oxford, where he adopted his Puritan beliefs and brought them to the New World. Sometimes he was an orphan raised by Franciscan monks, who may have taken liberties, which turned him violently against Roman Catholicism.

In any event, he thrived in New England, becoming a celebrated theologian, minister, educator and eventually the lieutenant governor of Massachusetts.

He was also an avid witch hunter. Just loved it, apparently. He presided over a record thirty-eight trials in Essex and Suffolk, and in each case the victim burned. One of the books contained an illustration. Alderhut—a Bible gripped in his hand, that same creepy smile, that same creepy necklace—stared without pity at a poor, terrified girl who was lashed to a stake. The flames lapping at her were reflected in Alderhut's eyes.

"You can almost smell it, can't you?"

Sam turned to see Ms. Lee nodding proudly at the illustration.

"The crackle of flesh, the charring of bones, the melting eyes . . . blood and marrow and bile boiling . . ." She smiled and took a deep breath as though recalling a childhood picnic.

Sam stared at Ms. Lee for a long moment, his lips slightly parted. "Ms. Lee," he said, swiping her cat Crowley off the table with his forearm, "I once woke up at the VA hospital to see the guy from the next bed standing over me with bloody pliers. When I asked him what was up, he said he'd just yanked all the fingernails out of his left hand. When I asked him why he'd just yanked all the fingernails out of his left hand, he told me he needed the ones on his right to play the guitar. That conversation freaked me out less than this one."

Ms. Lee grinned. "Surely as a military man you understand that violence is sometimes necessary to maintain order. Massachusetts was intensely prosperous during Alderhut's term and the crime rate was virtually zero."

"Well, unless you count setting innocent people on fire as a crime," Sam said.

"Who said they were innocent?" asked Ms. Lee.

"I think we can agree that they didn't know magic," Sam said. "That's what they were on trial for."

Ms. Lee chuckled. "Mr. Gregory, I have raised many children abandoned by West Cabot County. Do you know what

West Cabot County is? A cesspool. It is a dunghill of human excrement. And do you know why they rape, and take drugs, and steal and murder there with such abandon? Because they don't fear authority. You want to turn West Cabot around? Chain a few of those animals to stakes in the middle of town and set them on fire. And don't waste time asking if they're guilty of any one thing in particular because, Mr. Gregory, they're all guilty of something."

"I bet you don't get a lot of overdue books," Sam said.

Ms. Lee snorted and shook her head. "With soldiers like you, no wonder he lost the war."

Sam briefly considered force-feeding Ms. Lee her cat. And who in hell was "he"? Nixon? Add that allegiance to her charms. "I'm not a soldier. I'm a marine." He flashed the tattoo. "Semper fidelis, Ms. Lee."

"Oderint dum metuant, Mr. Gregory. 'Let them hate, so long as they fear.'"

Latin . . .

Where had Sam heard . . . ? Something about *Latin*.

"Caligula was fond of that saying," Ms. Lee continued, "and though I can't endorse everything about his leadership style—"

"Who's the head of the classics department?" Sam broke in.

20

THE STATUE

The campus cop escorted Harriet back to her room and told her to remain locked within until they sorted out the Paul situation. Harriet assured him that she had no intention of doing otherwise, then barely waited till he was off her floor before heading to the journalism department.

It was not that Paul's assault hadn't rattled Harriet. It was just that inaction always amplified her anxiety. That was because her seizures sometimes produced something called Todd's paresis, which at its most extreme left her completely paralyzed for up to forty-eight hours.

During these episodes, what unnerved her nearly as much as not being able to move were the snatches of sight and sound available to her. The top of a balloon, the squawk of a walkie-talkie, the shadow of a child, the rumble of a gurney, the moan of a patient—these glimpses were maddening in their incompleteness.

She had developed a pressing need to understand what was happening around her at all times. To fill in any blanks. This is what drew her to journalism. It calmed her to dig out a story.

She typed up her copy and dropped it in Mr. Chesterton's mailbox. She pictured him reading it and spraying a mouthful of Tab all over the offset printing press.

He had begrudgingly allowed her to pursue a story about bullying. She was coming back to him with a tale of steroids and a stolen book, and none of it was substantiated. Paul could have been lying when he said that Dale sold him his steroids. And the stuff about the stolen book was complete hearsay, based as it was on Sam's account of a conversation Laura had had with Dale. She was braced for Mr. Chesterton to print none of it and she wasn't sure she'd blame him. Who *was* that Sam guy, after all, and why should she believe anything he told her? *Witches?*

She knew the statue Sam was talking about, down by the dock. She'd walked past it many times but had never really looked at it. She stared up at it now. The bit of necklace carved under his cloak did seem out of place. She didn't think Puritans wore any jewelry (not that she knew much about them). Then again, maybe this was a medal for military service or some symbol of his office. Still—though maybe this was just Sam getting into her head—it had a pagan feel. Runic letters, animal glyphs . . .

And, she realized, she'd seen it before.

"What are you doing?"

Harriet jumped six inches without bending her knees.

Flynn frowned at her. "No boats till Friday."

"I was just taking a walk," Harriet said. She smelled the booze on him.

Flynn looked her up and down as though she might be trying to pull a fast one with this "walk" story. Eventually, he grunted and began weaving away.

"You ever looked at this statue?" she asked.

He stopped and turned. "It's kind of hard to miss."

"You see that necklace?" She pointed. "I never noticed it before."

Flynn glanced at it, then looked away quickly as though it pained him. "What about it?"

"Those symbols. Do you know what they mean?"

Flynn gazed over the water, slow-lidded, weaving. "How old are you?"

"Sixteen."

"You like this place? This school? You feel safe here?"

"Well, a football player tried to kill me earlier today."

This did not seem to shock Flynn the way she'd expected. He merely nodded. "Well," he said, "I don't know anything about anything. See no evil. Secret to my success." He started to stumble away again.

"A friend of mine told me Alderhut was a witch," Harriet said.

Flynn turned and ran his yellow eyes lazily over the statue. "Didn't end with him."

"What didn't?"

Flynn stared at the ground. He looked tired.

"Go home, dear." He turned and trudged away. "Lock your door and say your prayers." He snorted. "Fat lot of good that'll do." He twisted the cap off a flask and circled his palm above its neck. "*Hic est enim calix sanguinis mei,*" he mumbled. He drained the flask, then turned and whipped it at Alderhut. Harriet watched the flask clink off Alderhut's necklace and plunk into the sea.

"Hocus-pocus," Flynn slurred, then staggered off.

21

ET NE NOS INDUCAS IN TENTATIONEM

During his sophomore year, Bernard went with a church group to oppose a gay rights march in DC. He saw two men holding hands, screamed, "This is what God thinks of you!" and hurled his Bible at them. He missed so spectacularly that they were unaware that he'd even thrown something. The Bible landed in the street, where a car ran over it, defoliating its middle. Bernard retrieved the abridged Bible and returned to his squad's tent, where no one had noticed any of what had transpired.

The Bible remained on Bernard's bookshelf, the missing pages replaced with a private diary Bernard stashed there. At first, the diary had just been a list of names. These were

Bernard's enemies whom he meant to punish once he was in power. The list began generally (feminists, liberals, popular kids), but eventually began to name individuals, their infractions, and the punishment he deemed suitable ("Robert Soter/ wore a Carter T-shirt/flogging," "Stephanie Fazekis/rejected invitation to dance/electric shocks," etc.).

Of late, the diary had been augmented with photographs. These photographs were of girls Bernard knew. The girls did not, however, know Bernard. They might vaguely recognize him as a skulking, morose presence at the back of a classroom or in the cafeteria having lunch by himself, but they'd be hard-pressed to put a name to the face. Yet he had picture after picture of them in various states of undress: showering, drying their hair, talking, putting on makeup, struggling into and out of bras and panties . . .

"Sluts," Bernard whispered to himself with a hard *t* as his hand drifted into his pants. Filthy, filthy whores, he thought. These were exactly the types of jezebels his mother had warned him about. Beneath him in every way. They disgusted him. These pictures repulsed him every time he looked at them, which was several times daily. His face grew ruddy with excitement, his breathing rapid, his—

"Bad time?" Sam asked.

"JESUS!" Bernard said, lurching backward and toppling out of his chair. He tried to stand, but his pants, bunched about his ankles, tripped him up and he sat down heavily on the floor. He crab-walked away from Sam until he collided with a bookshelf. A few textbooks and picture frames rained down on him.

Sam picked up the diary and began paging through the pictures. He gave a deep, sad sigh and shook his head, tsk-tsking. "For shame."

"You're . . . how'd you get in my . . . what are you . . . Get out of my room!" Bernard squealed. "I'm calling campus security! I'm calling them right now!"

Sam smiled at Bernard and tapped the diary. "These girls are underage, Bernard. That makes this, among other things, child pornography. Still want to call the cops?"

All the color left Bernard's face. He looked as though he'd swallowed a handful of spider eggs and they'd just hatched. "Dale gave them to me!" he whined. "He put a hidden camera in the girls' locker room when he was on janitor duty! *He's* the perv!"

"And why would Dale give you these? You made it pretty clear you weren't buds."

"I don't know. I don't know why he does anything. He's a pervert."

Sam smiled. "Remember that stolen book I was looking for?"

"I don't know anything about that book, I told you."

"See, my mistake, I thought this kid Dale just stole it to

sell it," Sam said. "Turns out, he stole it to *use* it. Crazy-ass kid thinks there's magic in it or something."

"Fine. Okay. Whatever," Bernard said.

"Bit of a snag for Dale, though—book's in Latin." Sam picked up the books that had fallen on Bernard and returned them to the bookshelf. "According to Mrs. Schroeder, the head of the classics department, Dale doesn't take Latin."

Bernard folded his arms and nodded, his gaze darting everywhere as though he were following a fly buzzing about the room.

Sam lifted a trophy off the bookcase and squinted at it. "This one of the scholarship awards you said Dale drew a penis on?"

Bernard said nothing.

Sam polished the trophy with his sleeve and peered at it. "Oh, yeah, guess it is. You cleaned it up real good. I can only kind of make out the image of a dick on it." Sam read the engraving. "'Latin. First Prize. *Honor virtutis praemium.*' What's that mean?"

Bernard looked at the floor. "Honor is the reward of virtue."

"Not too many kids take Latin here, Mrs. Schroeder tells me," Sam said, "but you, you're like Dorkus Maximus. Top marks, reading and writing it like you're Julius Caesar."

Bernard remained totally still for a moment, then made a

mad dash for the diary. Sam blithely cuffed him in the jugular notch. Bernard staggered back and fell to the floor, clutching his throat and gasping for breath.

"You lied to me, Bernard," Sam said, "and that has put a strain on our relationship."

Bernard rolled over, coughing hoarsely. He swallowed with a wince. "I think you bruised my windpipe."

"These girls here," Sam said, "they won't give you the time of day. But then Dale says he's got pictures. And you can have them. All you got to do is a little extra Latin homework—translate this book—and for you, that's like Christmas, so why not?"

"You're crazy," Bernard said.

Sam picked up one of the framed photographs that had toppled off the bookshelf. It was of Bernard, before his growth spurt. A woman wearing a crucifix over a short-sleeved white blouse buttoned to her chin stood behind him. She gripped Bernard's shoulders and glowered into the camera. "Mother, I presume?" Sam said. "You have her scowl."

Bernard said nothing.

"She looks fun. How might she react to a call from the headmaster? No, it's not about his grades, Mrs. Sandoval. Young Bernard, you see, has taken an interest in, uh . . . candid photography. True, extracurriculars often look good on college applications, but . . . Gosh, this is hard. Which is how we found Bernard when he was—"

"Okay! All right, I . . . just . . . just stop. Please? Just stop. Just stop. Please."

Sam sat and drummed his fingers on the diary. "Where's Dale?"

Bernard slumped into a corner, kneading his skull with his fingers and rocking himself. "I don't know."

"You're getting on my nerves, Bernard," Sam said.

Bernard shook his head and talked into his chest. "I don't know! I swear to God, I don't know. I would tell you if I did, but I don't. I swear, I don't know!"

"What's he doing with this book?" Sam asked. "What *is* this book?"

"It's like . . . Satan-worshiping stuff. It's got spells and . . ." Bernard began to take deep breaths. "I think I'm going to be sick, can I please go to the bathroom?"

Sam kicked a wastepaper basket toward Dale. "You can puke in that. Book says you need some special necklace to cast its spells, right?"

"Yeah," Bernard said, surprised. "How'd you—"

"Anything else it says you need?" Sam asked. "Like some sort of special plant or dirt or scenic view or album played backward or any other bullshit that might point us in the general direction of where Dale took himself? I'm getting super-tired of looking for this kid, and you'd go a long way toward improving my mood, you gave me one fucking thing might be useful in finding him."

"I . . . I don't . . . I mean . . ." Bernard suddenly looked pensive. "Huh."

"Huh?" Sam said. "Huh what?"

"One of the spells," Bernard explained. "There's one that's supposed to summon a demon. You need to drink the blood of a small child."

A chill snaked up Sam's spine. The little kids in the masks who had made Sam buy a chocolate bar, they had said that their friend Izzy was missing. "Did you worry at all about how Dale might get a small child's blood?"

"I didn't think that he . . . that he seriously . . ."

"What?"

Bernard remained silent in the corner, broken and slack, staring at nothing.

22

THE TUNNELS

Among his other accomplishments, Mason Alderhut was a notable astronomer. In 1659, according to Zechariah Brigden's almanac, Alderhut designed "a perspective glass which shewed the Coelestial Motions of four satellites about Jupiter." At Danforth Putnam, Alderhut built the first observatory in New England, kept it state-of-the-art throughout his life and left directions that it remain so in perpetuity.

Thanks to this, the planetarium was the core of what was both the oldest and newest building on campus. It had been built up and over during the centuries, evidence of its former phases remaining within it like tree rings.

Earlier this year, after noticing that the Pleiades were not where they were supposed to be, Harriet had unscrewed the star projector mount and discovered, below the floor, some masonry with the same design she'd just seen on the necklace carved in Alderhut's statue: eldritch symbols, a feline eye . . .

If she looked closely, she could see bits of the same design etched onto the heavenly bodies in an antique model of the solar system designed by headmaster Laudon Mathers in 1796. The model was encased in a thick glass box by the lectern.

She thought of Flynn pelting the Alderhut statue with his flask.

Didn't end with him.

As president of the astronomy club, Harriet had access to Professor Memmer's desk. In it was a set of keys. Among these, she found one that unlocked the glass box over Mathers's solar system.

She discovered that the planets and the moons could be moved. She carefully rotated them, rearranging them like a jigsaw puzzle, until they resolved into the same image she'd seen on Alderhut's necklace.

The moment Harriet moved the last piece into place, she heard a click a few feet away. She turned and saw that a section of the tile was no longer flush with the rest of the floor. She stuck her fingers beneath the tile and pulled it back. A stone spiral staircase lay exposed, narrow and steep, corkscrewing into the belly of Danforth Putnam.

Harriet looked at the epilepsy bracelet on her left wrist.

Over the summer, she and Dr. Krasny had had an unpleasant conversation about driver's ed. Seizures could come at any moment, he'd said. He did not think it was a good idea for her to get behind a wheel. Ever. "When you think about it, you're lucky," he'd said. "You've got an excuse to let other people do the driving for you." She'd said she hoped Dr. Krasny was lucky enough to be in an iron lung one day, so that he'd have an excuse to let a machine do the breathing for him. That's when her mother had asked her to wait outside.

Harriet peered into the darkness below the hatch. If she were to have an episode down there, no one would know. This both frightened and excited her. She saw her disease as a bully and she liked doing things that said "fear of you will not rule me."

She wondered if maybe she should start letting it rule her *a little* when, halfway down the staircase, she heard the floor plate lock back into place. She thumbed her flashlight on, swept it around and saw that there were corridors heading in several directions.

The walls were covered with crude designs, like cave paintings. A man wearing antlers having sex with a doe. A hand with an eye in the palm. A giant horned demon, smoke curling from its nostrils, a human baby squalling in its open mouth.

She roamed for a while, exploring what amounted to a giant labyrinth sprawled beneath the campus. Years of D&D had honed Harriet's mapmaking skills and she carefully sketched the twists and turns in her journalism notebook.

She discovered that the underground tunnels connected large rooms, each of which lay below a campus building. Drawings within the large rooms gave clues as to what building was above.

In the room below the gym, imps played catch with a human head.

Below the cafeteria, witches baked children into a pie.

Below the old music building, rats followed a piper and gnawed the eyes from everyone in their path.

She was about to enter the room below the infirmary when she saw torchlight. She turned off her flashlight and silently backed down the tunnel from which she'd come.

The torchlight bobbed along the wall followed by a hooded figure with a necklace that twinkled in the light. He placed his torch in a wall sconce, then heaved a cauldron onto an altar below an inverted cross.

What Harriet had taken to be a hump in the man's back suddenly turned and croaked at her. The man cooed a few strange words to the frog on his shoulder while lighting a small blaze beneath the cauldron.

He uncorked a bottle and poured something thick and crimson into the cauldron, adding sprigs and powders from various pouches in his robe. Then he pulled a packet of wax paper from his pocket, unfolded it and revealed what looked to Harriet like a human heart. He plopped this into the cauldron, stirred it and sampled the brew.

He arched, head thrown back, chanting strange words. Harriet heard a clash of hisses as a number of snakes slithered out of nowhere and coiled around him. The snakes slid lovingly about his arms, chest and neck. He undulated rapturously.

The flashlight slipped from Harriet's sweaty grip and clattered to the ground.

He turned in her direction.

Harriet fumbled for her flashlight.

He rasped a few more strange words and pointed at her. The snakes slipped to the floor and headed toward Harriet, the frog hopping after them.

Harriet found the flashlight and ran.

She skittered past the room below the chapel, then grabbed at the room's archway to brake herself. She saw above her a spiral staircase like the one below the planetarium; she darted up it. It ended at a grate, which she rattled desperately, but it wouldn't budge. "Help!" she shrieked. "Open this! Please!"

Then she noticed something about the grate. She blinked and shook the tears out of her eyes so that she could focus. The grate was comprised of concentric circles etched with symbols she recognized. She turned the concentric circles until they formed the pattern on Alderhut's necklace.

The last circle clicked into place and the grate opened.

Something licked at her heel. She swiped at it and caught the frog in her hand.

She dove through the grate, rammed it closed and pushed an armoire in front of it.

She was in the chapel sacristy. As Harriet cracked open the door to the main altar, she heard Pink Floyd coming from the organ. Seven little kids in cloaks and papier-mâché masks danced and belted out alternate lyrics to "Another Brick in the Wall."

Father Ferreira shimmied through the choreography and sang along with them, his chasuble billowing like a sail.

> *"We don't need no foul temptation*
> *We have lots of self-control*
> *No pride, greed, wrath, envy, lust, gluttony or*
>   *sloth in the classroom*
> *Satan leave them kids alone*
> *Hey! Satan! Leave them kids alone!"*

Father Ferreira pinched his nose with a disappointed sigh and signaled the organist to pause. "Sloth? You've had this part for two weeks, and Wrath just stepped into the role today, so *what* . . ." He scuffed the stage with his tap shoe for emphasis, ". . . is your excuse for still not knowing all your dance steps?"

Sloth pouted enviously. Wrath smirked pridefully. Father

Ferreira spotted Harriet and began waving his arms as though calling someone safe at home plate.

"Excuse me! This is a closed rehearsal and the press is not invited! I remember all too well what you wrote about the Noah's ark play last year, Ms. Welsch, and I'm so sorry that our hard work left you 'rooting for the flood.'"

Harriet managed a shaky nod and staggered out of the chapel, her knees nearly buckling with the effort.

23

STORY TIME

Ms. Lee was sitting in a chair in the children's section of the library, a large old book open on her lap. Little kids sat quietly in a circle around her. "'If you wet the bed again,'" Ms. Lee read in a cheery, singsong voice, "'the Cellar Man will get you. But little Conrad did not listen. That night, as he lay in his bed, dreaming of creeks and warm summer springs, he wet the bed for a third time. Sure as night, the Cellar Man burst in! He was nine feet tall, wearing a frock coat made of ash and white gloves spun from spiderwebs. He sang: *"God in Heaven, what's that reek? This little cask has sprung a leak!"'*

"'Then the Cellar Man plugged the little boy up with a

cork! The boy began to swell like a feasting tick. He grew larger and larger and finally exploded all over the room! Little Conrad, now just a head, stared in horror at all the parts of him splashed across the floor, ceiling and walls. The Cellar Man laughed and danced a jig, the rat-bone buckles of his shoes gleaming in the moonlight, the tail of his powdered wig bobbing behind him. He sang: *"A bit of birdseed, that's the trick! The crows will clean this mess up quick!"'*

"'With that, the Cellar Man threw a handful of corn into Conrad's remains. Then the Cellar Man opened a window and whistled mightily. A murder of crows flew in and ate every scrap of the naughty little bed-wetter. The last thing Conrad ever saw was the crows plucking out his eyes.'" Ms. Lee closed the book and polished her reading glasses with a handkerchief. "I hope the moral of this story isn't lost on all of you. I'm looking at you, Roger Henderstock."

From the back of the room, Sam quietly said, "Wow."

M issing? Ridiculous," Ms. Lee said after ushering Sam into her office and shutting the door.

"So Izzy's here?" Sam asked.

"No, not currently."

"Where is he?"

"And what does this have to do with the missing book?"

"Where *is* he?"

"I don't like your tone," Ms. Lee said.

"Well, I suggest you get over that on the soonish side, Ms. Lee, since your insurance claim will be rejected if you don't comply fully with my investigation."

Ms. Lee sputtered and rolled her eyes. "Basic manners are, I suppose, too much to expect from the likes of you."

"Look, I'm sure you'd rather be reading some story about a kid who stutters getting his tongue nailed to a tree stump, but—"

"He's on the mainland being fostered by a couple considering adoption."

"How come his friends didn't know this?"

"Presumably because he didn't tell them," Ms. Lee answered.

"Why not?"

"I have no idea. Maybe he was afraid they'd be jealous. Maybe he was afraid he'd jinx it. Maybe he just thought it was nobody else's business. It certainly isn't yours."

Maybe not, Sam admitted to himself, but was that how ten-year-olds thought? Sam had met Izzy's friends, and they'd been worried about him. Small wonder, too. They weren't just his pals, they lived together, went to school together, endured Ms. Lee together. How likely was it that Izzy would leave without even mentioning it to any of them?

But maybe that was ascribing an unreasonable amount of

sentimentality to a ten-year-old in foster care. Maybe Sam was letting Harriet get to him.

He fucked with my friends. Do you let people fuck with your friends?

Is that why he was chasing this orphan now? To prove that he was worthy of that kind of loyalty? To feel whatever his young friend felt on her righteous mission, stalking through the woods in his coat, holy fire in her eyes?

"Can I talk to the couple fostering Izzy?"

"If you can find them."

"You don't know where they are?" Sam asked.

"We operate in the purview of the Massachusetts Department of Children and Families. They arrange placement with foster couples, not us. You are more than welcome to descend into that bureaucratic morass and see if they'll help you."

"Who picked him up?"

Ms. Lee closed her eyes and took a deep breath. She slapped the arms of her chair, launched herself at a filing cabinet and threw open its drawers, putting as much indignation as possible into her rummaging. She found a piece of paper and slapped it on the desk before Sam. "M. Moriah, license number 1079789."

"This M. Moriah," Sam said, opening his notepad. "What did he or she look like?"

Ms. Lee blinked rapidly and smiled. "Like a social worker."

―――――――

S am returned to the boathouse. Flynn was whistling merrily and polishing one of the boats with a chamois leather
cloth. He hadn't tidied up any since last they spoke. Parts of
at least three different meals still clung to his beard, and his
fingernails still looked as though he'd just dug his way out of
a collapsed coal mine. But there he was spit-shining his boats
as if they were about to be on display at a royal wedding.
Flynn caught sight of Sam. "The jarhead. What's up?"

"Three days ago, you pick up a social worker from the
mainland?"

"No."

"So then you didn't return a social worker to the mainland
with a ten-year-old boy?"

Flynn stared at Sam for a moment without moving. Then
he abruptly turned and made a beeline for one of the spearguns mounted on the wall of the boathouse. Sam drew his
piece and took the safety off.

Just beneath the speargun was a small metal desk. Flynn
gave the desk's bottom drawer a violent tug. Sam put the
safety back on and quietly reholstered his weapon before
Flynn noticed he'd drawn on him.

A Mr. Coffee rested on top of Flynn's desk. Old coffee
residue had so adhered it to the top of the desk that even
Flynn's vigorous rooting did not dislodge it. After a minute,

Flynn emerged with a logbook, which he splayed open before Sam.

"That's everybody I brought to and from the island in the last month. No social workers. No ten-year-olds." He snapped the logbook shut and tossed it back in the drawer.

"There a ferry that day?" Sam said.

"No."

"So help me understand how a social worker got to this island and left with a kid, not using any kind of boat?"

Flynn shrugged. "Maybe you got the dates wrong."

"Ms. Lee gave me the dates."

Flynn shrugged, spat into his cloth and worked a smudge off the chrome of one of his boats. "Maybe she got the dates wrong."

Or maybe it wasn't a social worker who'd picked up Izzy, Sam thought. Dale had worked for Ms. Lee and had been an orphan there himself. He could've learned exactly what the protocol was for discharging one of the kids into foster care. Dale had extorted some pretty big favors from Jimmy, Bernard and Laura. Suppose he had a grown-up on the hook, like a maintenance person Ms. Lee wouldn't recognize because they were too unimportant to look at. Suppose this person pretended to be a social worker, got Izzy and gave him to Dale, and Dale . . .

It was a lot of supposing. Dale's accomplice would have to have been over a pretty big barrel to steal a kid for him. More likely than not, Ms. Lee had just gotten the dates wrong and Sam was chasing his tail. He hoped so. At the same time, that left him exactly nowhere with this job, a fact that was beginning to wear on him.

"When was the last time you cleaned that thing?" Sam asked about the Mr. Coffee.

Flynn glanced at the coffee maker. "You doing the health department's job for them, too?" he said. He was now Windexing the mirrors on one of the boats.

Sam began to trudge away, then stopped and slowly returned. "You keep those boats awful clean."

Flynn glanced at Sam but kept working. "My job, isn't it?"

"It's just that you don't seem like a neat freak."

"Yeah?" Flynn said with a bored sigh.

"I'm looking for this other kid. Dale. Guess he's sort of the school's pot supplier."

"Uh-huh," Flynn said, squinting at a stubborn spot on a hood ornament he was addressing with a soft toothbrush.

"One thing's been bothering me," Sam said. "Where's this kid's pot coming from? I mean, how's he getting it on the island?"

Flynn stopped working and looked at Sam. He rested a forearm on the boat and raised his eyebrows, looking comically imperious given his ragged state.

"Boats, obviously," Sam said. "If they were my boats, though, boy, I'd keep 'em operating-room clean. I mean, it all goes fubar, Dale points the cops my way, I want to know they're not going to find so much as a seed."

Flynn stared at Sam for a moment, then roared with laughter. He took a swig from his flask and laughed again, the whiskey coming out of his nose.

"First off, that big landmass over there," Flynn said, wiggling his fingers at the mainland, "that isn't Mexico. There's no customs or drug-sniffing dogs or nothin'. Which is why anyone wanted to smuggle anything on or off this island'd just use the ferry. Second, bringing pot over from the mainland's not the only way to get it here. Look down. That stuff below your shoes? It's called dirt. Last I heard, marijuana's a plant."

24

THE CHESTERTON EFFECT

Harriet regaled Mr. Chesterton with her adventure in the tunnels. He listened, arms folded, exasperatingly composed. She wanted to open his stapler, grab his nose with it and squeeze until he yelped.

"Mr. Chesterton. I'm telling you that there are secret tunnels below Danforth Putnam designed for satanic rituals and I saw one being performed. This doesn't bother you?"

Mr. Chesterton sighed. He swiveled and looked at his bookshelf. He scooched his desk chair over to it, grabbed a volume and consulted the index. He found a page and read it aloud while rolling back to his desk.

"'In 1918, a series of tunnels were dug beneath Danforth Putnam, connecting all the buildings on campus. These tunnels carried coal-generated heat to the various classrooms and dorms. Eventually they became a conduit for steam pipes and electrical wiring. In the nineteen-sixties, the tunnels were designated a bomb shelter, and stocked with biscuits, water cans and painkillers, which disappeared during the nineteen-seventies. Since then, the tunnels have been locked and strictly off bounds to students.'"

He turned the book around and slid it toward Harriet.

"*Danforth Putnam: A History.* I recommend it if you have trouble sleeping."

"I saw a satanist—"

"Or a plumber. You said there were no lights down there."

"I had a flashlight."

"Which you turned off when the 'satanist' entered with a torch and snakes, which could have been a flashlight and cables."

"I saw an inverted cross—"

"Or two perpendicular pipes—"

"—and a cauldron and a human heart!"

"Which you saw from the next room. In the dark."

"What about all those drawings down there?"

"What about them?"

"Well, what are all those weird satanic drawings doing in tunnels for steam pipes and wiring?"

"They can't be worse than what I've seen drawn in the men's room stalls in the cross-campus library."

"This wasn't just graffiti! And since when do you need to unlock a two-hundred-year-old puzzle to enter a utility tunnel?"

"You don't. It was already open. An electrician forgot to reseal it. Your playing with that antique solar system model did nothing except possibly damage an antique solar system model. Seriously, Harriet, what were you thinking? You could get expelled for—"

Harriet grabbed *Danforth Putnam: A History* and rifled through it. She found a picture and stabbed it with her finger.

"What is that?"

Mr. Chesterton looked at the picture. "Mason Alderhut?"

"What's he wearing? Around his neck?"

"A necklace."

"Puritans didn't wear jewelry! It's not even a cross. Look how witchy it is."

"Witchy?"

"I think Mason Alderhut had some weird witchcraft cult here, and someone is trying to bring it back."

"And just out of curiosity, what does this have to do with Hello Day and/or bullying?"

Harriet pounded the desk in frustration. "I was chased by snakes!"

"You heard hissing. There are steam pipes down there."

Harriet violently unzipped her bag and plunged her hand

in. She pulled something out and plopped it on Mr. Chesterton's desk. "What is that?"

Mr. Chesterton grimaced. "It appears to be a frog. And I assume you've frightened it, because it just wet all over my crossword."

"This is what is called a witch's familiar, Mr. Chesterton! It is an animal trained to do the witch's bidding. I caught it! It's right in front of you!"

"Harriet, please. I want you to see Dr. Beckett."

"I'm not crazy!"

"I know you're not," he said gently. He looked at her with such concern, she wanted to brain him with his typewriter. "But you just had a seizure *and* an attempt on your life. Anyone would be reeling from that."

Harriet crossed her arms and stared intensely at her forearms.

"I think you may be experiencing something called posttraumatic stress disorder. They used to call it shell shock. A lot of soldiers get it. It's nothing to be ashamed of. But it is something you should talk to Dr. Beckett about. Come on, I'll walk you. On the way there, we can chuck this poor thing back into the woods."

He attempted to lift the frog with his soiled newspaper, but Harriet snatched it, stuffed it back in her bag and marched to the door. She swung around to face Mr. Chesterton.

"Mr. Chesterton! The only reason Nixon isn't president anymore is that Ben Bradlee stood by Woodward and Bernstein!"

"Well . . . and term limits . . ."

"Someday! Someday I want to know what it's like to have an editor who has my back!"

"Let's go see Dr. Beckett."

"I don't need you to escort me to Dr. Beckett's office. I know the way. And unlike you, Mr. Chesterton, I am not afraid to follow a path where it leads!"

She stormed out. Mr. Chesterton, predictably, remained inert.

25

EVAN

S am repeated the rundown for the twentieth time.

"Izzy Kurban. He's ten years old. He was being raised at Danforth Putnam. According to their records, he was delivered to a social worker, M. Moriah, license number 1079789."

True to Ms. Lee's prediction, Sam wasn't having a ton of luck with the Massachusetts Department of Children and Families. Anyone Sam managed to reach had three questions. The first was if he was related to Izzy in any way. The second was if he was law enforcement. The third was if he would please hold.

It was only after Sam claimed that he was Izzy's uncle

and a police lieutenant from Astoria that anyone refrained from transferring him, and even then it was just to inform him that they couldn't give out any information about a child in the system.

"Not even to a relative?" Sam said. "And a cop?"

"I'm sorry, Officer, but not without a court order. Did you want to request a hearing?"

"Sure," Sam said. "Meanwhile, could I at least get a phone number? I just want to hear my nephew's voice, make sure he's okay."

"Again, and I'm sorry, but a judge would have to okay that. We have to protect the privacy of the child and his foster parents. Do you have any reasons to believe he might be unsafe?"

Sam closed his eyes and mopped his face with his hand. He blew a smoke ring at the ceiling and answered. "Yes. I'm worried that a demented teenager might have abducted him so that he could drink his blood in a demon-summoning ritual."

As Sam expected, the next thing he heard was a dial tone.

Sam went to the student jobs office and looked up Dale's work record. Dale had spent a lot of time doing janitorial assignments but had also logged a fair amount of hours landscaping. His supervisor during those occasions was a grounds-keeper named Evan Stahl. With the shadows lengthening, Sam picked his way through the forested acreage surrounding the campus, looking for Evan's cabin.

Eventually, Sam discovered a small shack. A hammock was strung between two poplars outside it. A shovel leaned against one of the trees next to a pyramid of beer cans.

"Evan?" Sam called, rapping on the door to the shack. He poked his head inside, and the stench nearly dropped him. It wasn't just the reek of pot that had settled indelibly into the shag rug, the curtains made from a bedsheet, the small sofa kept together with duct tape and everything else in the room; it was the collision of this aroma with several cans of air freshener, presumably deployed to cover the scent of weed. He left the shack, calling out into the woods, "Evan!"

Out of the corner of his eye, Sam noticed that the hammock was swinging. He also noticed that the shovel was now missing. He heard a twig snap behind him, turned and met the shovel square in his face.

*A*nd he was back in Vietnam. He was wearing fatigues and holding a rifle. Gunfire and shouting all around him. Something exploded thirty yards from him and he narrowly rolled out of the way as what was left of a jeep flew over him. The lieutenant was signaling a retreat. As they fell back, fissures began to open in the ground. Sam saw the members of his platoon swallowed up, one after another, by the suddenly appearing chasms.

STEPHEN LLOYD

He broke into a sprint, desperate to outrace the crumbling earth, but a mortar blast knocked him headlong into a widening crevasse and he fell, down, down, down, toward an endless river of lava. . . .

S am jerked awake. He was on his back outside Evan's shack. His hands were trussed behind him with an extension cord, his feet lashed together with a belt. He guessed from the throbbing that there was a nasty cut above his left eye.

Staring down at him was a skinny, leathery man with long, matted hair and a Creedence Clearwater Revival Bad Moon Rising T-shirt so faded that it mocked its formerly psychedelic hues and, like the man wearing it, seemed on the verge of falling apart. He hopped from foot to foot, shaking his shovel like a deranged gravedigger. "What are you, like, the DEA?" the guy asked.

"No," Sam said calmly. "I am not the DEA. You're Evan, I'm guessing."

"You're the fucking DEA, aren't you?"

"Again, no."

"Kid sold me out, didn't he?" Evan said, his voice rising in pitch. "Well, you got nothing, man! Go ahead, search, there's nothing!"

For a long moment neither of them said anything.

"Kind of hard for me to search when I'm hog-tied, Ev," Sam said finally. "And what is it you think I'm looking for?"

"Kid said you DEA guys," Evan went on, "you need a big-profile bust for your quotas and you'd hang me out to dry for nothing, and those plants, you know, who knows who planted them. Back in the day they used to grow 'em for rope, they grew wild anyway, people planted them or not, and this place has been around a long time, no saying those plants are mine."

"I don't care what you're growing," Sam assured him.

"I ain't growing shit!" Evan protested. "Jesus! Why you putting words in my mouth?"

"Hey, come on, let's calm down, okay?" Sam said.

"School property and all," Evan continued to ramble, "they're going to string me up, the kid said. I should probably kill you, bury you out here, who's even going to know, kid said."

"This kid we're talking about," Sam said, "he got a name?"

"You know, I got a nervous condition," Evan continued. "You would, too, things I've seen. And how a man unwinds, you know, privacy of his own, not hurting nobody, I don't deserve to get screwed for that just 'cause you have a quota."

"I'm not a cop, Evan. If I were, I'd have a badge. Do I have a badge?"

"Well, I don't know what's in your pockets, man."

"Take a look. Not like I can stop you. You'll see a business card says I work for an insurance company. I can't arrest anybody. What's more, you help me out, I'll see to it you get paid for your trouble."

After a few moments' consideration, Evan tentatively approached Sam and knelt down to empty his pockets. Sam jackknifed up and headbutted Evan in the nose, then pulled his knees up and kicked Evan in the chest with both feet. Evan tumbled backward and dropped the shovel. As he staggered to his feet and groped for the handle, Sam worked his tied hands down his body, brought them under his feet, then rocked forward and jumped up, ducking just as Evan's shovel sang through the air above his head. His hands still tied together, Sam lunged forward, grabbed Evan's shovel by the shaft, twisted it out of Evan's grip and smacked him on the head with it. Evan teetered for a moment, then sank to his knees and fell face-first in the leaves.

Evan came to a few minutes later and realized with alarm that he was tied up. He realized with greater alarm that Sam was standing over him, holding the shovel, and that he looked really, really pissed. Evan's eyes welled up. "Oh, man. I am so screwed," he said.

"Nuh-uh," Sam said, shaking his head. "This is barely first base. Screwed is a long way around the diamond."

Evan began to cry. "I don't deserve this, man. I'm a good person."

"Sorry, what?" Sam asked, clearing out his ear with a pinkie. "My ears are ringing a little from when you hit me in the face with a shovel. Last thing I heard clearly was you saying you should kill me and bury me in the woods."

"I never would have, man, I never would have!" Evan insisted. "I'm peaceful, I'm all about that. I just . . . It's panic, man. I been way on edge lately and that fucking kid got under my skin, convinced me you guys were going to lock me up and throw away the key, and I'm not going to be able to handle, like, an incarceration deal, I'm just not, it's going to be like a disaster to my mental health and my—"

"Shut. The fuck. Up," Sam said.

Evan stared up at him silently, eyes wide.

"I got some questions," Sam said.

"Oh, man, everything," Evan said, quaking. "Everything. Whatever you want to know. And I know I'm in no position to ask for favors, but one of the brews from my fridge would really help me not freak out right now."

Sam wasn't feeling particularly charitable toward Evan at the moment, but the guy looked about one loud noise away from crapping himself, and that was not going to make the afternoon any better, so he pulled a Bud from Evan's mini-fridge, popped it and held it to Evan's lips. Evan drained it so quickly that Sam thought the can would crumple in on itself.

Evan smiled gratefully and burped. "'Scuse me. Um . . . you want to do a bowl?"

"No," Sam said.

Evan looked at Sam hopefully. "Can I?"

"This kid who got you all worked up and fixing to kill me," Sam said. "What's his name?"

"Dale," Evan said. "Don't remember his last."

"Don't need it," Sam said. "What's your relationship with this kid exactly?"

"I'm, like, his supervisor when he pulls gardening detail."

"That it? You never see him outside his student job?"

Evan fidgeted. "Well, you know, we got to be friends doing that. Now he comes around, once in a while, has a beer."

"He's seventeen," Sam said.

"Yeah. What? I mean, I have a beer. He has, you know, juice. Or, like, Ovaltine," Evan said.

"You hang out with a lot of seventeen-year-olds, Evan?"

"Well, who else am I going to hang out with? I live on, like, high school island."

"Right, why does Dale hang out with you?"

Evan stared at Sam and swallowed. "I'm . . . you know . . . a good conversationalist."

Sam smiled, drove the shovel into the dirt and rested his arms on the handle. "Really? Show me."

"What?"

"Here, I'll be Dale," Sam said. "I'm tired of the boring, immature drivel my classmates usually say. I want the rich, deep thoughts I get from the brain-dead hippie who lives in a toolshed with his beer can collection. Share."

"You're freaking me out, man," Evan said, his eyes beginning to water again.

"You grow pot and he sells it," Sam said. "That's the answer to 'what's your relationship with this kid, exactly?'"

Evan turned pale. "It was the kid's idea, man, I swear," he almost yelled. "I mean, cards on the table, I had a few plants, purely for personal consumption. He's the one comes and says he's going to turn me in unless I start growing product for him. I mean, look around, man, I look like some sort of kingpin? I look like a guy with a lot of disposable income? I don't even have a color TV—"

"Okay," Sam said.

"I got a sixteen-inch black-and-white—" Evan said, nodding with disgust toward his shack.

"Okay,"

"Doesn't even get UHF, it's like I'm in *The Flintstones* or—"

"Stop talking!" Sam said. Evan did. "Where's Izzy?"

Evan frowned. "Who?"

"Ten-year-old from the orphanage."

Evan looked convincingly bewildered. He stared at Sam, wide-eyed, cocking his head like a confused puppy. "I mean . . . occasionally they bring 'em out here for field trips to learn about nature or such, but . . . Is one of 'em lost? What's he look like?"

Sam studied him. One thing he was pretty certain of by this point was that Evan did not have nerves of steel. Sam did not believe that Evan, braced with the name of a child he'd helped to abduct, could play it this cool. He decided to switch gears.

"Dale mention a book?"

"A book?" Evan repeated.

"Yeah, an old, valuable book got stolen from the library, had stuff about witchcraft in it, maybe Dale said—"

"No way," Evan said, impressed. "He got their book?"

Sam stared at Evan. "What do you know about this book?"

"Well, I mean, not much per se, but I seen someone say spells and shit."

Sam blinked. "Say that again?"

"Look, I told you I seen some weird stuff, and now we're on the subject, it's *that* you DEA guys should be looking into and not me."

"What do you mean you saw someone say spells and shit? What did you see?"

Evan explained that since, prior to Dale's extortion, he had never grown pot for anyone but himself, he was ill-equipped, operating out of his humble shed, to fill the demands of Dale's growing business. Dale had insisted, consequently, that Evan transplant his smokables to the Devil's Vale.

The Devil's Vale was a dark, overgrown hollow on the east side of the island, so named because Alderhut had burned people there. Several protected plant and animal species flourished in the Devil's Vale, which made it a legal headache for the school to cultivate, so the whole area grew wild. Some of those plants and animals were also poisonous, so the school had simply cut off the vale from the rest of the island with an electrified fence festooned with warning signs.

Dale had argued that the off-putting natural hazards of the vale, its junglelike density and its threatening fence, made it a place one could grow rows and rows of cannabis with little fear of detection. So they'd located a section of the fence that was particularly remote and almost completely hidden by brush, made a work-around circuit with jumper cables and cut through it. A few months later, they were harvesting their first crop.

The whole operation had played havoc with Evan's already fragile nerves. He lived in fear of being caught, of being thrown in prison, of being raped in prison, and worst of all, of being without pot, the one thing he'd come to rely on quite heavily, he admitted, to quell his anxiety. He'd started biting his fingernails down to the quick, his hair had started falling out and every morning his hands were numb from squeezing them into fists while he slept. He hadn't thought he could get any more tense, and then, one night, while he and Dale were doing a little moonlit gardening, they'd heard someone in the vale with them.

Evan had wanted to run as fast as he could out of there but found that his legs would not oblige him. The next thing he knew, Dale had yanked him to the ground. Dale had put his finger to his lips, grabbed a shovel and begun belly-crawling toward the sound. When Evan did not follow, Dale had prodded him with the shovel and jerked his head toward the intruder. Evan was scared of a lot of things, but none more than Dale.

Dale had gently pushed away some leaves and in a clearing twenty yards away they'd seen someone in a hooded robe arranging candles in a five-pointed star and lighting them. The hooded figure had read something strange and foreign to Evan's ears from a small, distressed-leather book, its spine and face covered with weird, "witchy-looking" symbols. Then the hooded figure had tossed a few pebbles into the center of the flaming pentagram, pulled a bullfrog from its pocket, and slit the bullfrog's throat, spilling its blood over the pebbles. The hooded figure had then bent, touched "this weird necklace it was wearing" to the pebbles, and the pebbles had turned into rubies.

"After that," Evan concluded, "all Dale could talk about was getting his hands on that book 'cause he wanted as many rubies as there were pebbles and he sure didn't mind killing a few frogs."

Sam listened quietly to Evan's tale, and when he was certain it had concluded, he gave Evan a patient smile. "You and Dale saw this?"

"You're damn right we did."

"And Dale went and stole what he somehow deduced was the, uh, spell book from this unidentifiable, black-arts type who for some reason kept this magic book in the library?"

"Kid's on janitor detail in the library," Evan explained. "Said he saw the headmaster take it out once to show it to these, like, big visiting muckety-mucks from China. Knew right away it was the same book. Didn't tell me he was planning to steal it, but damn, I'd like to know how to turn rocks into rubies. Wouldn't you?"

Sam nodded thoughtfully. "So when they're warning kids at this school about the dangers of recreational drug use, do they just show them you?"

"Hey, don't tell about what we seen," Evan begged. "I don't want any trouble."

"With the witch, warlock, frog hater, whatever the hell it is you 'saw' in the dark after God knows how much drug consumption?" Sam asked. "Yeah, don't worry. Your secret is safe with me. Not sure I can say the same about your idiot teenage partner once I find him. At least now I've got an idea where to look. Which way to the Devil's Vale?"

26

PENITENTIA

It was early evening in Danforth Putnam, and all was quiet outside Cabot House, one of the freshman girls' dorms. A hedge in its empty courtyard began to shudder and from it emitted the sound of gnashing. This was Bernard, feeding. He lifted his face to the moonlight, which slid glossily across the sticky remains clinging to his maw and off the giant Reagan button, now hanging upside down from a patch of torn sweater. Half a dozen crumpled wrappers were strewn at his feet. Bernard added another to the pile and tore into a fresh candy bar, adding to the riot of chocolate on his face, his pimples and everything else in this world be damned.

Through a second-story window, Bernard could see two

girls jumping up and down on a twin bed, their budding breasts bouncing beneath their pajamas.

Bernard's sense of who he was had disintegrated. Dale had jiggled it and Sam had popped it, like a great soap bubble, massive and shining within Bernard's psyche—its vast dimension revealed to be surface, angstroms thick, and concealing no inner structure, no depth, nothing. He was hollow, had always been hollow, and now felt it, his ego having blown apart like dandelion spores in a child's breath. He had no convictions left, no pride, just feral will, grunting in the bushes as he wolfed down chocolate and masturbated to two fourteen-year-olds hopping on a mattress.

He watched numbly as a sudden burst of wind picked up the candy wrappers and set them swirling about his feet. He looked up at the school flag and noticed, with surprise, that it lay limp and unmoving. He looked back at the wrappers still settling by his shoes.

One of the girls pulled down the shade of the second-story window. Cursing, Bernard fought his way out of the hedge and began trudging back to Hastings House.

He avoided walking on the campus and took instead the long way through the woods. He wanted to be cloaked in dark and untamed nature, wanted the embrace of the wild and pathless. He closed his eyes and fancied himself a jackal or a wolverine, the predator unseen, stalking and fearless. With a teary smile, he bayed at the moon.

As if in response, the wind picked up again. It carried the sound of large, flapping wings. Bernard lifted his head and spun in circles, looking for some enormous bird or bat, but saw none.

Ahead of him, a maple was swaying, its red leaves falling from it in clumps. As he neared the tree, he realized that it was not swaying but shaking in spasms as though a creature were astir in its highest branches. Moving closer, he heard the snap of twigs, that same flapping sound and a faint serpentine hiss. When he got to the foot of the tree, he craned his head, squinted at the upper limbs and screamed.

Bernard sprinted back toward campus but did not get far before something landed directly in his path. He stared at it, into the eyes of it, as urine coursed down his leg. His hand was shaking so severely that he could barely work it into his pocket to remove the silver cross his mother had given him. He held it before the thing and began to shriek tremulously, *"Adjúro ergo te, omnis immundíssime spíritus, omne phantásma, omnis—"*

Something sliced out, shearing through the cross, Bernard's fist and both his cheeks. Bernard howled, his cheeks parting in a grotesque, yawning smile. He loped away, trying to hold his face together with his good hand while blood spurted from the other. Before long, his knees buckled and he began to crawl, sputtering. He felt the ground fall away as something lifted him up into the fiery reaches of the red maple.

No one saw the branches of the tree shake. No one heard

Bernard's muffled shrieks grow hoarse and finally cease. And no one heard the sound of those terrible wings.

A werewolf snarled, the full moon hanging low behind it. A woman screamed and ran. The image began to roll and Evan whacked the set. This failed to improve the picture. He switched off the TV in disgust, shook *American Beauty* out of its sleeve and fired up his record player. He took an extremely long drag on a skull-shaped bong as "Box of Rain" washed over him. He'd broken out his private reserve and was on track to make quite a dent in it. "Yeah, you're tough, right? Fuck you, tough," Evan mumbled as he performed a little air karate and took a pull from a pint bottle of Jack. "Fucking kill you, man. Don't know who you're messin' with. DEA fuck. You don't know a thing about me." He tugged at the collar of the temple garments he still wore.

Evan had grown up in Provo, Utah, one of nine. His father had been a farmer and an elder in the Mormon Church. While trying to remove a stick from a combine head, his dad had lost a finger and screamed "My word!" At the time, that was the closest thing Evan had ever heard to swearing.

The church sent Evan to California as a missionary when he turned eighteen. They might as well have sent him to Zambia for all the cultural references he shared with most of the population. Still, he doggedly tried to interest anyone he could in the gospel, knocking on front doors, chatting up pedestrians, standing outside movie theaters as they emptied, offering pamphlets and a smile.

He was strolling down Venice beach in his black slacks, short-sleeve white shirt and black tie, amiably swinging the Book of Mormon in his hand, when he happened upon a clutch of beatniks. A bearded lad in a beret was reciting some foulmouthed "poetry" while his pals snapped along.

Evan asked if they'd heard of Joseph Smith or the angel Moroni.

"I grew up in Pasadena. It's full of moroni," one of them said. The others tittered.

"I want to hear," said a redhead in a tight black turtleneck and sunglasses.

So Evan told them about the sacking of Jerusalem by Nebuchadnezzar, about the flight of the Lamanites, Jaredites, Mulekites and Nephites, and how the Nephites eventually fell into wickedness and were slain by the Lamanites.

The redhead eyed him quietly during all this, slowly nibbling on a big red apple.

It was a cool day. He doubted it was more than 65 degrees, but he found himself sweating. He'd never seen anyone eat an apple like that. It seemed almost cruel, as though it were prey she was putting through a protracted death.

They invited him for coffee. He demurred, explaining that his faith forbade it. Along with tobacco and spirits.

"You poor dears," the redhead declared. "You can't drink, you can't smoke, you can't dance . . ."

"That's Baptists," Evan corrected. "We can dance."

"Prove it," she said. She kicked off her shoes and starting shimmying in the sand. Someone started playing the bongo drums. Evan felt the pull of something behind his navel. He shuffled toward her.

Evan had understood dancing to be square dancing. He did not understand the undulous motions of this strange woman. She twisted her hips as her knees sank to the sand, slowly drawing her hands across her face as though casting a spell. The waves crashing behind her seemed to get larger and louder, booming with each unsettling thrust of her body.

Obviously, she was a witch. How else to explain his taking a swig from the hip flask she pulled from her garter, or getting into her car, or following her into the pool house of some Malibu residence he was fairly certain wasn't hers. Or his fornicating with her. Three times.

Evan was silent as she drove him back to the mission. He went into a white-hot panic when he saw the temple. "We have to get married," Evan blurted out to her.

She gave him a kindly pout. "Sorry, sport. Someone beat you to it." She took a wedding ring out of the glove box and slipped it on. "And unlike you people, we're only allowed one at a time."

He felt like he'd had a stroke. "You're married?" he squeaked.

She squinted and tilted her hand in a *comme ci, comme ça* gesture. "Neither of us takes it all that seriously. Sometimes I have a guy on the side. Sometimes he has a guy on the side."

He really wished she would just run him over and be done with it. Instead, she gave him a hug and a fake phone number and left him by the side of the road.

He skulked in the shadow of the temple until well after dark, pacing the sidewalk, crying, pounding his forehead. He eventually walked to the YMCA. The next day he found a job as a dishwasher. It was a month before he got up the nerve to write letters home. The first was to his father. When he received no reply, he wrote to his mother, then to each of his siblings. None of them ever wrote back.

He felt like a tightrope walker watching the carefully knotted ends of his rope unspool and fall away. He was dizzy with dread. He turned to booze (though, to this day, he avoided coffee).

His craving for fellowship led him to many groups—Buddhists, Theosophists, Hare Krishnas, one biker gang—but he just couldn't stay put and found himself slowly meandering north along the coast. It was in an ashram in Oakland that he discovered weed.

The Grateful Dead played Boston University in November

of 1970. It was Evan's first trip back east, and it was there that he saw the job listing for groundskeeper at Danforth Putnam. He took it as a sign.

"Now the LORD God had planted a garden in the East, in Eden; and there he put the man he had formed," Evan muttered to himself while he sucked on a sugar cube laced with LSD. Maybe this was how he was meant to find his way back. At any rate, it came with room and board and his girlfriend at the time had just kicked him out of her van.

Needless to say, it had not proven his way back. And it sure as hell wasn't Eden. If anything, it was Gehenna, where he was doomed to suffer for his wickedness, tormented by pricks like Dale and now that asshole from the DEA.

How had he come to be so divided against himself? Why had God split him so? *"Zwei Seelen wohnen, ach! in meiner Brust,"* he yelled at the ceiling. It was the only German he remembered, taught to him by a grandmother he assumed was now dead and wouldn't speak to him even if she were alive. There was no way back. He knew that now. He himself had barred the way.

There was a loud thump outside his shack. The pint bottle slipped from Evan's hand and he bobbled it, emptying most of the whiskey onto his T-shirt. He stared at his door for a long time. His heart was just beginning to slow when he heard an even louder thump. He stood up so quickly, his feet left the ground and one of his Birkenstocks fell off. He grabbed a bread knife and stepped out of his shack.

His hammock was swaying. In the hammock was a dark lump. Evan sucked down what was left of the whiskey and chucked the bottle. He put the bread knife in his belt, pulled the shovel out of the dirt where Sam had left it and approached the lump.

As he got closer, Evan could see that the lump was a wad of clothing. He put the tip of the shovel beneath the clothing and slowly lifted it. As the clothing unfurled, Evan could see what was left of a shredded shirt spattered with blood.

As Evan stared at the bloody shirt, Bernard's glasses fell into the hammock. Evan looked up into the tree from which the glasses had fallen. He saw something else fall and land with a wet slap on one of the tree's lowest limbs. It was Bernard, what was left of him, hanging in strips. Evan screamed.

Then he heard something with huge, powerful wings descending.

Evan turned and saw it land. It was so still. Only its wings moved, and they as gently as a resting butterfly's. It was boring into him with those horrible eyes—windows to nothing—just red-hot coals. He swung his shovel at it. The thing caught the shovel and tossed it, with Evan attached, twenty feet. Evan landed on his shoulder, which separated with a crunch.

His eyes filled with tears and he couldn't catch his breath. He took the bread knife from his belt and limped away, caroming from tree to tree.

The thing landed in front of him. Evan threw his knife at it. Almost as soon as the knife left his hand, it was flying back at him and with a splintering force pinned his hand to a tree trunk, buried hilt-deep.

The thing just stared at him as Evan tried to pull the knife from his hand. He eventually gave up and then dangled from it, semi-crucified, as he slipped into shock.

Evan stared back at the thing, his lids getting heavy, all of him growing cold and numb. The world was losing its color. "You just going to leave me like this or—"

There was a sharp whipping sound, but Evan never heard it. Blood began to bead along a seam running down the middle of his forehead, through the bridge of his nose, then his chin, then his sternum. His left half gently cleaved from the right and slipped, neatly severed, to the ground.

27

DR. BECKETT

D r. Beckett wanted to make absolutely certain that people knew he wasn't "square." He had a beard, wore flip-flops and used words like *grock* a lot.

In soothing tones, he talked to Harriet about stress, the power of suggestion, the mind's reaction to trauma, and the "little short circuits in her brain," which was his cute way of describing her epilepsy. She endured this quietly, nodding along, because interrupting him would only prolong his patronizing lecture and increase the likelihood that she'd flurry him with one of his Bataka bats.

She was not new to therapy. Because no one had been able to find any physical explanation for her seizures, she had spent several years on this couch or that, analyzing dreams, staring at inkblots, screaming through puppets or at empty chairs. It had achieved nothing. She still had seizures anyway. This predisposed her to regard psychology as a pseudoscience founded by a coke-addled quack, and she had little patience for its practitioners.

"Can I ask what keeps croaking and moving around in your bag?" Dr. Beckett asked.

"A frog," Harriet explained.

"Your pet?"

"A friend's."

"Dig," said Dr. Beckett, nodding. "You know, what's interesting about frogs, like a lot of animals, they have an amazing ability, almost a biological imperative, to find their way home."

Harriet perked up. "Really?"

"Oh, yeah. They'll cross all sorts of terrain to get back to their familiar habitat."

So many animals, Dr. Beckett went on, will reject an unfamiliar environment in favor of a familiar one, even if the unfamiliar environment is better. "We like repeating patterns, even unhealthy ones. You feel me?"

Harriet smiled and nodded. For the first time since the session began, she wasn't tempted to wing one of Dr. Beckett's Baoding balls into his neck. He'd managed, inadvertently, to be helpful.

28

THE DEVIL'S VALE

Despite Evan's barely coherent directions, Sam found the Devil's Vale and the section of electrified fence Evan and Dale had bypassed with jumper cables. He crawled under it and began hacking his way through the overgrowth, down into a deep hollow. Fog rolled into the hollow off the Atlantic marine layer and billowed out into the moonlight so that Sam felt as though he were disappearing into the maw of a giant, panting hound.

Visibility was not good, and he stumbled around in the fog for an hour without finding anything. He was about to give up and try his luck come daylight when he heard a voice. He slowly moved toward the sound and began to make out a teenage boy—naked, sitting on the ground, his back to Sam.

The boy was muddy, covered with scratches and sitting in the middle of what appeared to be a pentagram, raked into the earth with a stick, its angles marked by burning candles. Surrounding the pentagram were the carcasses of several small animals and a discarded box of salt. The boy babbled to himself quietly and made smacking noises with his lips.

"Dale?" said Sam.

Dale turned at his name, a relaxed smile on his face, which was covered in blood. He held the remains of what appeared to be a squirrel in his hands. The necklace Laura had made him jangled against his bare chest.

"Very angry," Dale said in the tone of someone telling a story at a cocktail party. "I hugged him. He became my dad. 'Shocked?' he asked. I was, for whatever reason. He was naked, hairy, his skin a bit gray, even mottled, like a leper or zombie." Dale took a dainty bite out of the squirrel.

"Dale," said Sam, walking up to the boy.

"A tiger entered and began eating eggs the jester had been playing with," Dale continued cheerfully, "conjuring from magic tricks or having been laid by his bird."

Sam crouched down by the boy. "Dale," he said again, staring into Dale's unfocused eyes. The kid was out.

"I tried to focus on the tiger, to summon its energy," Dale continued.

"Dale!" Sam shouted, trying to wake him.

"Miss Anna, Miss Anna, Miss Animus, animus, animus, animus, *animus nocendi*," Dale babbled on.

Sam clapped loudly in front of Dale's face until he finally came to. Dale slowly focused on Sam, then jumped, wondering how he'd gotten where he was.

"Wakey, wakey," Sam said.

"What . . . what," Dale started to say, then noticed the squirrel in his hand. He dropped it and began screaming hysterically. Sam reared back and slapped him, twice. Dale stared at Sam, petrified.

"Nice to finally meet you, Dale," Sam said. "Big fan of your work."

"What . . . I'm . . . Who are you?" Dale asked.

"Greta Garbo," Sam responded. "Where's Izzy?"

Dale stared at him blankly. "Who?"

"The kid from the orphanage. Any of this his blood?"

Dale looked genuinely baffled, squinting at Sam and forming words with his mouth, but speaking none.

"There's nobody out here but me, man," he finally said. "I don't know an Izzy. This blood . . ." He stared down at the squirrel remains. "Jesus Christ . . . I ate a squirrel." He turned his head and vomited.

Despite the fact that he was staring at a nude teenager covered with vomit and animal blood, Sam felt relieved. He did not see anything that could have been Izzy's corpse. It appeared Dale had sacrificed a squirrel, rather than an orphan, in whatever weird ritual he was attempting. Maybe Izzy really was on the mainland, starting a new life. If so, he was well shut of this place, Sam thought.

"I'm here to get the book back that you stole."

Dale looked at Sam. "You're that cop dude."

Sam sighed impatiently. "I'm not a . . . just . . . Where the hell is the book, Dale?"

Dale shivered. "I can't tell you."

"Wrong answer."

"I need it," Dale whined.

"For what? To cast spells to make better-tasting squirrels?"

"To protect myself," Dale whispered.

Sam kneaded his forehead wearily. "From what, Dale?"

Dale shivered. "The demon."

"The demon." Sam sighed. He lit a cigarette. "Summoned a demon, did you?"

"No, *I* didn't," Dale said.

"Really don't have time for this, buddy," Sam said.

"It was probably whoever Evan and me saw in the woods that one time."

"Oh, right," Sam said. "You and Evan saw someone using a magic book to make sapphires or something out near your pot crop."

"I think it was rubies."

"Fine, and now you think this wizard slash jeweler summoned some sort of demon to come after you?"

"Yeah!" Dale screamed. "And not just me! Anyone who knows about the book, and that includes you, fuckface!"

"Well, gosh," said Sam, "better get that book and start casting some demon-go-back-where-you-came-from spells but quick. I'll grab it for you. Where did you put it again?"

"You think this is a joke?" Dale rasped. "I saw it."

"Good for you." Sam sighed. "Is the book here? I mean, obviously it's not on you. Nothing's on you. And speaking of which, want to put on some clothes, champ?" He looked around for a hiding spot. The hollow of a tree maybe? Under a bush? He really didn't want to start rooting around in the dark since he remembered the warnings on the fence and didn't feel like getting bitten or stung or infected with poison oak or whatever other crap they had out there.

"I saw it," Dale said, fighting back tears. "I went to talk to Jimmy about what he told you and how we were gonna . . ." He swallowed hard. "This thing was ripping his insides out."

"You saw *what*?" Sam asked.

Dale told him about the monster gutting Jimmy in his bathroom.

"I talked to Jimmy last night—*late* last night—and aside from his brain, he seemed very alive," Sam said. "Also, no one's mentioned a kid getting disemboweled in his bathroom. Seems like something would have hit the grapevine."

"I saw it," Dale said.

"At night. From a roof. Through a window," Sam said.

175

"And forgive me if I'm making assumptions about a pot dealer sitting naked in the woods with a half-eaten squirrel, but were you stone-cold sober at the time?"

"It happened!" Dale shouted. "I mean, like, I could throw up thinking about it!"

"Well, that's saying something for a guy with your diet," Sam said, pointing at the squirrel. "And a pentagram filled with salt is supposed to protect you from this thing? Why, it have high blood pressure?"

"I'm just doing what it says in the book!" Dale yelled. "You think this is what I wanted it for? I wanted to do cool magic shit, like make rubies out of stuff, and hypnotize girls! I didn't want to be sitting out here in the jungle, sacrificing little animals and hoping it wouldn't end me!"

"So that's it?" Sam asked. "Your plan is to just sit here butt naked until, what, the monster gets bored and goes away?"

"No, I think . . . I think I worked out how to control it."

"Well, that's a relief," Sam said. He noticed that a low-hanging leaf was starting to blacken near the flame of one of the candles in the pentagram. "Hey, how 'bout we put out the candles before you start a forest fire." He grabbed some dirt and started dousing the flames.

Dale squealed in panic. "What are you doing! Stop it! Jesus! I need that to help control the monster!"

"You are really working my nerves, kid," Sam said as Dale

pulled out a book of matches from somewhere and started to relight the candles. "Knock it off."

Sam shoved Dale away with his boot. Sam saw a corner of plastic sticking out of the dirt. He stooped to touch it and Dale scrambled to stop him. Sam casually caught Dale by the face and pushed him onto his back. Sam tugged at the plastic and unearthed a sealed baggie. Inside the baggie was an ancient leather book. "Hallelujah," he said. He stuffed the baggie in his jacket pocket and headed away.

Dale hobbled after him. "Wait! Stop! Where are you going?"

"To return this book, and then the hell away from this fucked-up prep school," Sam said.

"I need the book!" Dale shrieked.

"No, Dale," Sam said, marching toward the mouth of the hollow as Dale scuttled after him. "You need a shower, some clothes and a couple days in the infirmary, probably, for exhaustion, dehydration, exposure and whatever squirrel blood has done to you. You do *not* need—"

A rock sailed into the base of Sam's skull. He stiffened, then crumpled to the ground, lights out.

Dale spun in circles looking for the source of the rock. A monster emerged, almost noiselessly, from behind a tree. Then the cologne hit Dale's nose.

Paul peeled off his werewolf mask. "That's right, bitch." He spit on Sam.

Dale scooped up the book, the candles and the rest of his necromantic paraphernalia and bolted deeper into the vale.

"The hell are you going?" Paul asked and ran after him. "We need to strategize."

"Uh-huh," Dale said, looking around nervously as he ran.

Paul jogged behind him. "I went to smack around that Jimmy guy like you asked, but I couldn't find him. I guess he blabbed to this little Black nerd girl, though, 'cause she knows you're my connection. I tried to scare her into keeping her mouth shut, but then this asshole—hey, are you listening to me?"

Dale finally found what he gleaned was a suitable spot and started remaking his pentagram.

"What are you doing?" Paul asked. "Listen, if they come to you, we need to get our stories straight. I am not getting kicked off the team for this. I've worked too hard."

Dale squinted at Paul. His words had a dreamlike quality. He understood them, but they made no sense in the current context.

"Football? You're worried about football?"

"You're fuck right I'm worried about football! A coach from Notre Dame parked a Mercedes in front of my grandparents' house. It was in my name. This is my life."

Dale was lighting the last candle when he heard its wings.

"The hell is that?" Paul said, turning toward the sound.

Dale took the book out of the baggie but was trembling so much that he dropped it. The flapping grew louder. Leaves and branches snapped right behind him. He heard a low guttural hiss.

"Holy shit," said Paul.

Dale grabbed up the book and thumbed through it until he found the incantation he was looking for. Clutching his medallion, he said what he hoped were the magic words.

The flapping stopped.

Dale slowly turned. There it was. Staring right at him but not moving. Not attacking. Not doing anything. He let out a long, slow, shuddering breath and started laughing. Tears filled his eyes. He was safe. He had beaten this thing. Better—

It was now his. And, boy, did he have plans for it. There was a long list of people he was going to introduce to his new pet. Starting with—

Paul, lemur-eyed and panting, whispered, "What is that?"

Dale smiled at the creature. "Kill Paul."

"What?"

Paul's puzzled frown remained on his face as his head rolled to Dale's feet. The rest of Paul crumpled to the ground, spurting.

"I am so glad I never have to smell that gross aftershave again," Dale said, punting Paul's head away. "And now—"

Dale's face exploded in a tangle of blood, bone and flesh.

He was falling again.

His legs jerked him awake. He opened one eye, then the other. Oh, that fucking kid, Sam thought. He was going to kill that fucking kid.

He staggered to his feet way too quickly, grabbed a tree to stop the earth from tilting out from under him and puked. The pain started where the rock had hit him in the back of the skull and radiated all the way down to his shoes. "Dale!" he shouted as he headed into the woods.

Twenty minutes later, Sam was still swatting his way through bushes and branches, yelling Dale's name and cycling through every curse he knew. His boot hit a slick patch and he went down on his ass. He lay on his back, stared up into the heavens and thought about all the other things he could do with his life besides chasing naked teenagers with stolen books.

Then he saw it, splayed open, spine up, lying in the dirt: the book. Sam stood and grabbed it as something wafted past him: the plastic baggie.

"Dale?" he called upwind.

Sam shoved the book into his jacket pocket, started in the direction the baggie had come from and almost slipped again. He looked down and saw that the ground was covered with a red mulch, much of which had gotten on him when he fell. The mulch was streaked as though something had recently been dragged through it. Sam followed the drag marks to where they disappeared into dense brush just behind a V-shaped poplar. He tentatively parted the brush with his hands.

Dale's mutilated body stared up at him, one eye gone, his lower jaw missing, and his entrails ripped out. Sam realized with horror what the red mulch he'd slipped in was. Neatly piled next to Dale were the parts of what had recently been Paul.

A snake darted out of Dale's eye socket and hissed at Sam. Sam sprang back, slipped again on Dale's innards and slammed the back of his already punished head against the V-shaped poplar.

29

THE FAMILIAR

Kapui, when he was not playing D&D, destroying people at chess or studying, was tinkering in the electronics lab. He got very excited when talking about something called ARPANET. Apparently, this was something the Defense Department used to link computers together, but (thanks to something called CSNET) it was being expanded to involve civilians, and Kapui said it wouldn't be long before anyone with a computer could connect to it over normal phone lines.

Harriet didn't know anyone with a computer, didn't know why you'd want one and didn't know why, if you had one, you'd want the military to have access to it, but she was not going to rain on Kapui's parade, especially when he was willing to loan her a Nagra recorder and tape a tiny microphone to the back of a squirming frog. God bless Kapui. He didn't even ask her why she wanted it.

It was Harriet's hope that Dr. Beckett was right about frogs and that this one would lead her to her hooded friend. It was certainly possible that Dr. Beckett was full of crap, that this frog would relish its newfound freedom and disappear into the woods. Then she would be no closer to discovering who had been down in the tunnels and would owe Kapui a new radio mic.

"The signal will get stronger"—he tapped a dial with a needle flickering under it—"the closer you get to it. But stay close. If it gets more than five hundred feet away from you, it'll be out of range."

She walked to the infirmary, roughly above the spot where she'd first seen the frog in the tunnels, unzipped her bag and set it free.

At first, it just sat there, staring at her. Then it took a few unhurried hops, circled, stopped where it started and stared at her again. Dr. O'Megaly nearly stepped on it as she was leaving the infirmary.

"Harriet? Why aren't you in your room? I thought— gah!"

Dr. O'Megaly's frenetic two-step seemed to get the frog moving and it darted off at speed.

"Sorry, Dr. O'Megaly, my frog's getting away!"

It wasn't that fast, but it was small, and the sun had gone

down. The frog kept disappearing in the high grass off Salem Street. Pretty soon, Harriet lost sight of it completely. She watched with alarm as the signal needle on the Nagra grew fainter and finally flopped to rest. She continued in the same direction for a couple of minutes, but the needle stayed dead. If it had snuck back this way, she would have seen the needle move, she reasoned, so it must have juked left or right. She went with her gut and headed left between the laundry and the archaeology building. She was about to give up the frog for lost when she saw the needle twitch.

She used the signal strength to home in on the frog, which appeared to have settled down, at least temporarily. She couldn't see the frog, but over the Nagra headphones she could hear its intermittent croaks.

The strengthening signal drew her to the side of a building she knew well.

She entered, padded up some steps and followed the signal into a classroom.

The frog was ribbitting at a padlocked locker. Harriet stared at the locker, breathing hard. Then she ran out of the building to a gardening shed. She stole some hedge clippers and ran back. She clipped the padlock and opened the locker. The frog hopped into the pocket of a hooded robe hanging within.

"Harriet?"

She turned to see Mr. Chesterton, holding a newspaper, his mouth slightly open.

"Did you just break into my locker?"

The weight of the frog caused the robe to slip off its hanger. Dangling behind it was a necklace Harriet recognized.

Harriet stared at Mr. Chesterton. She was trembling and the hedge clippers in her hands drummed against the locker door.

"I'm going to have to report this," Mr. Chesterton said. "And why aren't you in your room? Did you go see Dr. Beckett?"

He moved toward her and she raised the hedge clippers.

"Harriet. What are you doing?"

The hedge clippers shook in her outstretched hands like a divining rod.

"Put those down," he said.

The frog took this inopportune moment to hop out of the locker and streak across Harriet's field of vision, startling her. Mr. Chesterton seized the opportunity to snatch the hedge clippers roughly away from her. She lurched as she tried to hang on and then fell to the ground next to the offset printer.

Mr. Chesterton loomed over her, holding the clippers.

"Are you on drugs? What is the matter with you?"

Harriet scooched away from Mr. Chesterton.

As he bent to grab her, his tie swung forward and dangled

between the wheels of the offset printer. At the same moment, the frog hopped onto the power button.

The drums of the printer violently grabbed Mr. Chesterton's tie and yanked him in. He flailed for the power button but could not reach it. His knees buckled as his chin collided with the rollers. Harriet saw the panic in his eyes as his face began to purple. She heard a sickening crunch as his neck broke. He quivered for a moment, dropped the hedge clippers, and then drooped, his glasses carried away and mangled by the still rotating drums of the printer.

Harriet stared at him, unable to move. The churn of the printer built to a roar and everything went white.

30

MISSION ACCOMPLISHED

*M*en were wearing hooded cloaks and mumbling in Latin, their heads bowed in prayer.

One of the men pushed back his hood. It was Mason Alderhut. Another man pushed a small, mangy boy wearing rags for clothes before Alderhut. The boy stumbled and fell, his hands trussed behind him with rope.

Alderhut drew a large knife from his belt, and the boy began to quake. Alderhut cut the ropes tying the boy and helped him to his feet. He smiled at the boy, gently brushing the dirt and tears away from his sunken cheeks with the backs of his massive fingers. Then he grabbed the boy by the hair and slit his throat, quickly bending him over a basin that caught his blood as he jerked and flailed.

The blood flowed from the basin into several cups. Alderhut raised one of the cups and drank. His adherents followed suit.

Alderhut turned to Sam, raised his cup and said, "Welcome to the New World."

S am's eyes snapped open and he jackknifed awake, feeling around for his rifle. Dr. O'Megaly eased him back onto a cot, saying, "You're okay, you're okay." Behind her, Headmaster Arundel stared at Sam with concern.

"What happened?" Sam asked.

"Security guards found you passed out in the Devil's Vale," the headmaster said. "What were you doing out there?"

"I . . . somebody killed Dale."

"What?" said the headmaster.

"And that other kid, the big one. His . . . Wait, the guards didn't see their bodies?"

"Their . . . No," said the headmaster, flummoxed. "Who killed Dale? When?"

"It . . . I . . . Hold on, I passed out two feet from their bodies. I was covered in their blood. No one saw that?"

Dr. O'Megaly and the headmaster shared a concerned look.

"Sam . . . there was no blood on you." The headmaster pointed to a mirror. Sam looked at his reflection and was shocked to see that not a trace of Dale's gore was anywhere in evidence.

"They found you just like that," the headmaster said.

Sam stared at them, at a loss. "I was . . . How . . ."

Dr. O'Megaly shone a penlight into Sam's eyes and began moving her finger back and forth. "Follow my finger with your eyes," she said. "Can you tell me who the president is?"

"Stop," Sam said, pushing away the penlight.

She began feeling his head and hit a tender spot.

"Ow," he said, pulling away.

"How'd you get that lump?" Dr. O'Megaly asked.

"I don't know."

"You don't know?"

"I've been hit in the head a few times, but I didn't imagine . . ." Sam remembered something. "Wait . . ." He looked around and saw his jacket hanging off a chair. "Hand me that."

Dr. O'Megaly obliged. Sam reached into his jacket pocket and removed the small leather book. "I'm not imagining this, am I?"

The headmaster stared at the book for a moment in utter shock, then took it reverently. "How long have you had this?" he asked.

"I got it from Dale just before he got killed. Well, and then, after—"

"You saw him get killed?" the headmaster asked.

"No, but when I came to—"

"When you came to?" Dr. O'Megaly asked.

"I . . . Someone hit me in the head with a rock and knocked me out. When I came to, I saw two bodies. What was left of them."

"And that made you pass out again," Dr. O'Megaly said.

"No, it didn't make me . . . it startled me, and I slipped in . . . *Dale* and hit my head on a tree."

"So that's twice you've been hit in the head hard enough to knock you out in the last twenty-four hours," Dr. O'Megaly quietly pointed out.

Three, if you counted Evan's shovel, Sam thought, but he didn't think mentioning that would help his case.

"Is it possible," Dr. O'Megaly said gently, "that you got the book from Dale, he knocked you out, and you woke up here?"

"That's not what happened," Sam said.

"You touch any plants while you were out there?" she asked.

"Well, yeah."

"There's a species of angel's trumpet that grows wild out there. It can cause hallucinations if it gets into your bloodstream," she said. "In fact, there's a lot of poisonous stuff out there. We might want to do some blood work, make sure you're not—"

"Just send someone out there to look again," Sam said. "Both those kids are still missing, right?"

"Actually, no," said the headmaster. "Dale's aunt called to say Dale showed up on her doorstep saying he'd dropped out."

"What?" said Sam. "How'd he get off the island?"

"The caretaker at the boathouse said someone stole one of the motorboats," the headmaster explained.

Sam just stared, looking from one to the other and hoping one of them would say something that vaguely conformed with his perception of reality. Nothing about finding Dale's body felt like a dream or a hallucination. There was nothing disconnected about it, no odd suspensions of the laws of space and time, and it stuck to his memory the way dreams did not. Sam's dreams never lingered; they tiptoed out of the bedroom first thing in the morning, and by the time he got in the shower, he couldn't remember anything about them. He remembered every second of what had happened with Dale. Still, given everything they were telling him, it was possible, he guessed, that it had all been in his head. He sure as hell wished it were.

"And the Incredible Hulk?"

"We're still looking for Paul Spitz. But no one saw his body next to you in the woods, Sam. It's possible he left the island with Dale."

"I'm going to get something to help you relax," Dr. O'Megaly said and moved away.

The headmaster smiled at Sam. "Seems like we caused you quite a bit of trouble, Sam, and I'm sorry." He raised the book. "But thank you for finding this. It means the world to us to have it back. Now, you get some rest, give the doctor a chance to make sure you're okay. Then we'll send you home." He gave Sam a reassuring pat on the shoulder and left.

Dr. O'Megaly returned with a pill and a glass of water.

"What's that?" Sam asked.

"Valium. And after the day I've had, if you don't take it, I will."

The meds Sam was on, she may as well have been handing him a Life Saver, but he took it anyway. "Thanks," he said.

"Now let me see that cut above your eye," she said. As she leaned over to examine the cut, Sam saw the chain of a necklace visible under her collar.

"What's under your blouse?" he asked.

"Feeling better already, I see," she said.

"No, the . . ." Sam delicately lifted the chain with his index finger and brought the necklace outside her clothes.

Dr. O'Megaly smiled. "Brigid of Kildare. One of the patron saints of healers. Can't hurt, right?"

Sam suddenly felt very tired. He wanted to surrender to the hospital mattress beneath him and let this pretty doctor, who smelled fantastic, take care of him. Instead, he heard himself ask, "Dale's got an aunt?"

"Guess so," Dr. O'Megaly said as she cleaned the cut over his eye.

"But he's here as a ward of the state," Sam said.

Dr. O'Megaly shrugged. "Not all family is, you know, family."

"Family enough that she's this kid's first stop after he gets off the island," Sam said. "And she's the uptight, upright type who calls Dale's school the second he shows up? He's got that kind of family in his life? Anybody heard of this aunt before now?"

"Don't know," Dr. O'Megaly said. "Don't know who talked to her."

"And what were security guards doing out in the Devil's Vale?"

Dr. O'Megaly shrugged. "I think if there's a short in the electric fence, they know someone's tampered with it and go check it out."

"Dale had this work-around with jumper cables," Sam said. "He's been going in and out for months. It stopped working tonight?"

"Your first time going through tonight, right?" Dr. O'Megaly said. "Maybe you nudged something. Or maybe they were just out there looking for Paul."

"And this motorboat thing," Sam said, pushing himself up on his elbows. "I went to the boathouse and every boat was locked up tight. I told the guy there's a kid might be looking to nick one of the boats. That's when he decides to get lax with security?"

Dr. O'Megaly smiled. "Guy who runs the boathouse, Flynn, drinks a fair bit. Not what you'd call reliable after lunch."

It was a nice smile. Sam liked that smile. He wanted to stay there and bask in it. Wanted to see if this hot doctor, who had to be starved for adult companionship, would enjoy the company of a bright, handsome, world-traveled marine. Making time with this sweet, sexy brunette with a smoky voice and a prescription pad, that sounded like heaven. He waited until she was at the other end of the hall, then he spit out the Valium and left.

"Your problem," he told himself as he headed back to the Devil's Vale, "is that you can't leave well enough the hell alone."

31

PETIT MAL

Mr. Chesterton kept a bust of Athena over his door. She was a symbol of freedom and democracy, he explained, and it was their job as journalists to protect both.

The frog sat on Athena's head, staring down at Mr. Chesterton, whose blue face still danced on the rollers of the printer. His tie still whined against the pressure of the drums, the tip of it flapping like an ululating tongue.

Harriet stared at nothing. She blinked. Then blinked again. A spasm went through her and she inhaled as though she'd been underwater for a full minute. She struggled to her knees, slapped the power button off, lurched toward a trash can and vomited.

She worked the hedge clippers under Mr. Chesterton's chin and severed his tie. He slid slowly to the floor. She turned him over. His eyes were bulged and bloodshot, his tongue lolling out of his mouth like a cartoon wolf. She pressed two fingers against his carotid artery but found no pulse.

She noticed she was missing her glasses. She spotted them under a desk, bent to retrieve them, then sank to the floor and curled into a ball like a pill bug.

She breathed into her cupped fists, quivering, letting sweat and tears pool around the ear she had pressed to the floor. "Get up," she told herself. "Get up. Get up. Get. Up. Just keep moving." She slowly rolled to her knees and used the desk to pull herself to her feet. She looked around and spotted Mr. Chesterton's locker. She remembered what she'd seen inside and threw it open. The robe and the necklace were still there.

She noticed a gap between the edge of the locker's rear panel and its right side. She put her fingers into the gap and realized she could slide the rear panel left like a pocket door. Behind it was a stone wall. Carved into that was a design made of concentric rings.

She heard the crackle of a walkie-talkie and then footsteps. A flashlight beam hit the blackboard. It raked across the frog, which croaked and leapt off Athena.

A security guard entered. His flashlight found Mr. Chesterton. He fumbled for his walkie-talkie and yelled for help.

He swept his flashlight around the room and saw the hedge clippers and a locker that—maybe it was his eyes playing tricks on him—had just closed itself. He edged toward it, noted the clipped padlock next to it and opened it. A frog stared up at him.

32

ASHES TO ASHES

Sam wandered for a good while until he saw the V-shaped poplar again. This time, he realized it was actually two trees—one white, the other black—but growing so close together that they appeared to stem from a common trunk split at the roots.

There was no longer a body in the dense brush behind the tree, and the ground was no longer slick with Dale's insides. But the soil, he could tell, had been turned. And there was a conspicuous tidiness to the area. All around it, there were fallen leaves, bird droppings, squashed berries, broken twigs— but in this one spot, only fresh-swept earth as though the wind had decided to blow just this patch clean.

A fly buzzed by Sam's ear, and he crushed it against his

neck. He began circling the area in a widening spiral, hoping to pick up tracks.

He heard a great flapping. A shadow fell over him. He looked up to see a giant crow tilt above him and take a branch, a worm in its mouth. The bird stared at him, its eyes glossy gold in the moonlight, its head inclining here and there with a clockwork twitch. Sam knew little about birds, but he thought crows were smaller than this, and as he drew closer, he wondered if this might be a raven. "Nevermore," Sam said.

The worm in the bird's mouth caught Sam's eye. If Sam knew little about birds, he knew even less about worms. Still, he was fairly confident they didn't have a fingernail and what was left of a knuckle. The bird swallowed the finger in its beak and flitted off. Sam followed, hoping it might lead him to the source of this grisly fare.

Soon, the flies grew thicker, their buzzing gathering in a dull roar. The swarm was focused on the contents of a freshly dug pit. Sam drew his gun and silently edged toward it.

Within the pit, lying in a grotesque tangle of limbs, were parts of Jimmy, Laura, Bernard, Evan, Paul, Dale, and a very young boy who Sam gathered was Izzy, the orphan. Sam heard a twig snap and rolled into a defensive crouch behind a tree.

Someone was humming cheerfully. A hooded figure walked to the lip of the pit carrying a canvas bag. The cat, Crowley, darted about the person's feet.

Sam primed his gun. "Freeze."

The hooded figure turned abruptly in his direction but otherwise obliged.

"What have you got in the bag, Ms. Lee?" Sam asked.

The librarian pushed the hood of her cloak back and smiled at Sam. She shook Paul's head out of the sack and into the pit.

"There a reason you killed all those people?" Sam asked.

"They saw the book," she said. "Except for Izzy. His death served a different purpose."

"And what was that?" Sam asked.

Ms. Lee's mouth twitched. She appeared to be suppressing a laugh.

"You drink his blood to summon a demon?" Sam asked.

She nodded.

"Do you have any idea how batshit, fucking crazy you are?" Sam asked.

"You served your purpose, Mr. Gregory, recovering the book and leading us to all the uninitiated who'd seen it, but now it's time for you to go."

"Us? Who's us?" Sam asked.

She clutched her medallion and began mumbling in Latin.

"Ms. Lee, you are three or four abracadabras away from me emptying my .45 into you, so why don't you knock this shit off and tell me who the hell—"

She flicked one of her fingers. Sam's gun sailed out of his

hand as though she'd tugged it with an invisible string. It clattered against the trunk of a tree fifty feet away.

"Please watch your language," she said. "This is, after all, a school for children."

Sam stared at her, frozen. Ms. Lee pushed her palm toward him, and an invisible force knocked him head over heels. He scrambled to his feet and saw her grinning at him with all the wide-eyed wonder and warmth of a baby. Then she lifted off the ground and beamed down at him, the moonlight behind her. He tore off toward the mouth of the vale, her rolling, delirious laughter spurring him.

33

COVEN

Harriet huddled on the spiral staircase that led from the journalism building into the tunnels. She put her hands in her mouth and bit down to stop them from shaking. She wasn't sure why she'd run. She hadn't killed Mr. Chesterton. His frog had killed him. But she imagined explaining that and decided she'd been right to dash.

What . . . what if she'd lost her mind? What if she'd imagined everything in the tunnels?

But she had his robe and that necklace. She'd seen him down here doing . . . something. Hadn't she?

She took out the map of the tunnels she'd begun to make and started plotting a path back to her dorm. If she got into her room, she could think. She could figure out what to do next.

Lock your door and say your prayers. . . . Fat lot of good that'll do.

Why had Flynn said that? What did he know?

She was walking—she thought—beneath Washington Irving Place, when she saw a candle. Someone in a hooded robe was using it to light the way. She killed her flashlight and pressed her back against the wall.

From the other direction, she heard shoes scraping stone. She turned and saw another hooded figure with a candle. It was headed toward her.

She moved quietly away, took a right and pulled up short when she saw two more hooded figures with candles. In the other direction, three more. She squatted, fished around in the broken masonry and found a loose brick. She stood and held it high.

The hooded figures began to converge. But not on her. They all seemed to be heading in one direction, away from the main campus. Harriet quietly pulled Mr. Chesteron's robe and necklace from her bag and put them on. She found a candle and some matches in one of the robe's pockets. She lit the candle, threw the hood over her head and slowly fell in with the throng.

34

ROUGH WATERS

Sam ran, skidded, and tumbled back to the mouth of the vale. He'd just cleared the fence when, in the distance, he saw a dozen tiny flickers slowly snaking toward him.

Soon he could see that the flickers were candles, that each candle was held by a person wearing a hooded cloak like Ms. Lee's, and that they were making their way toward the vale, the eerie chords of their mumbled chants just reaching him. He sprinted through the narrowing gap between the candle bearers and the fence and cut toward the dock.

He jimmied open the door to the boathouse, cranked up the bay wall, jumped into a motorboat and began bringing a rock down on the chain mooring it.

The door banged open. Flynn stumbled in and fired a

speargun at him. Sam ducked and the harpoon missed him, lodging near the boat's motor. Flynn charged, loading another harpoon, as Sam danced backward in the motorboat, inadvertently kicking the starter. Flynn fired another harpoon, which barely missed Sam and splintered the paneling by the throttle.

As Flynn reloaded, Sam charged, hoping to tackle Flynn before he could raise his weapon. The buffeting of the boat threw off his jump, however, and he ended up landing ribs first against the edge of the dock. He turned his head and was staring up the shaft of a locked and loaded harpoon.

"I know what you is," Flynn slurred. "I know what goes on here."

"I'm not . . . I'm not part of this," Sam said. "I don't—"

"Go to hell," Flynn said, but as he started to pull the trigger, the motorboat kicked into gear and the chain pulled taut, taking Flynn's legs out from under him. He fell on his back, his head over the edge of the slip, but he miraculously held on to the speargun, which he continued to level at Sam.

At the same moment, Sam saw the lever for the winch suspending the sailboat above Flynn. He dove for it and slapped open the catch. The boat came crashing down on Flynn's face, snapping his neck over the lip of the dock.

Flynn's limbs still twitching, Sam went through his pockets and found a large ring of keys. He opened the lock on the chain mooring the already moving motorboat and dove in as the chain spooled free.

As he pulled away from the dock, Sam saw several of them standing on the bluffs overhanging the bay, hoods thrown back, medallions against their chests. He saw the headmaster and Ms. Lee and Dr. O'Megaly and a dozen others, their hands joined, chanting.

The waves began to churn around Sam, and soon he was awash in roiling froth. He threaded his arms through the steering wheel to avoid getting thrown clear as the boat was tossed airborne by the chop. The waves were driving him back against the shore and the small motor in his boat was no match for them. They dashed his boat against the breakwater; he spilled out and hit the rocks, then all was black.

35

THANK YOU FOR YOUR SERVICE

When Sam came to, he was sitting in the middle of a pentagram. Dale's pentagram had looked like a child's version of this one. The candles dotting each angle were three feet tall, set on thick silver sticks filigreed with golden fractals and inlaid with rubies. The pentagram wasn't raked into the ground with a stick but chiseled into a giant stone slab, its crevasses overflowing with a mélange of exotic spices. Gouged into the stone were what appeared to be great claw marks.

Surrounding Sam was a throng, all wearing hoods, all chanting, their heads bowed. One of them stepped forward and lowered his hood. It was Thomas Arundel, the headmaster. He smiled.

"Hello, Sam."

"What the hell is this?" Sam asked, standing.

"A faculty meeting of sorts," the headmaster said. "We've been having them here since the school was founded over three hundred years ago."

"Uh-huh. And what are you meeting about?" Sam asked.

"You," said the headmaster.

"How did Ms. Lee . . ." Sam started, then trailed off. "Who are you people? What's going on? How did you . . ."

Sam stared into the headmaster's wide, friendly face—a face with which the headmaster had learned to evince warmth over the centuries. But the eyes still twinkled with giddy cruelty. It was Mason Alderhut.

Sam tried desperately to pull himself together. This was a trick. This was all some trick. The stuff Ms. Lee had done in the forest, the way they'd summoned the waves to crash his boat, the headmaster looking like Alderhut—this was all just a magic trick, and he was not going to fall for it.

"I can kill some of you," Sam shouted. "Maybe not all, but if you come at me, some of you are going down. You all want to take that chance?" He gathered some of the spices in one hand. He thought maybe he could blind whoever came at him first and make a run for it.

"We're not going to kill you, Sam," the headmaster said.

"Oh. Right," Sam said, glancing at the claw marks. "You're gonna have your demon do it. The one you murdered that poor kid, Izzy, to summon. That's what I'm supposed to think?"

"You don't understand, Sam," the headmaster said.

Sam eyed the thick silver candlesticks, thought maybe he could use one as a weapon. "I understand you're a creepy group of psychos, and I also understand that there's no such thing as demons!" he yelled. "I don't know how you're pulling this magic shit, but I know it ain't real!"

"You don't understand, Sam," the headmaster said again.

"Come on, bring on the demon! What, does one of you wear a costume? You got a giant dog you dress up? What kind of Scooby-Doo bullshit is this?"

"Sam," the headmaster said kindly, "you are the demon."

"What?"

"There is no Sam Gregory," the headmaster said. "We created him. We had to. Without giving you the anchor of a mortal ego, you would be impossible to control, even for us."

Sam stared at the headmaster, slack-jawed. "Right . . ." he said. Sam edged a little closer to the headmaster, thinking he might be able to get him in a chokehold and that if he threatened to snap his neck, maybe the others would back off.

"I know," said the headmaster. "You think you know who you are: Sam Gregory. Insurance investigator. Veteran of a war where you got that tattoo."

The headmaster pointed at Sam's snake tattoo. In the undulous candlelight, it looked as if the snake were slithering.

"In fact, you *are* a veteran of a war, Sam. The first war of all time." The chanting grew louder. "It was between God and Lucifer. And your side lost."

One more foot, Sam thought, just get one foot closer to me, you crazy bastard, and I can—

A searing pain shot through Sam's shoulder blades and he dropped to his knees gasping. "The fuck did you do to me?" Sam rasped.

"Nothing, Sam," the headmaster said quietly. "You are as God made you."

Sam wailed in agony as the skin around his toenails and fingernails split and blood ran down his feet and hands. His gums cracked and blood filled his mouth. Unendurable pain rippled through every muscle in his back. Something was tearing its way out of him. He heard a slow, booming, flapping sound and smelled feathers wet with blood. The candle flames around him flinched and faltered in a rhythmic breeze, and Sam realized with horror that the breeze came from him. He turned his head and saw, over each shoulder, a mass of leathery sinew and black feathers eight feet high. He stared at the razor-sharp whip of a tail coiled around his cloven hooves and the black talons that had sprouted from his fingertips. He tilted back his head, parted his fangs and howled in terror.

"Time to go home, Sam," the headmaster said.

This isn't happening, Sam thought. They'd given him something to make him hallucinate. Or this was just another nightmare. Or . . . he'd finally snapped. He knew he was on the edge. He remembered the way the doctors had looked at him when he got back from the war, how he'd lied to get released, didn't tell them about waking up in the corner of his room with his gun in his hand, or pissing his sheets, or the meds he went to four different pharmacies to fill. Maybe he'd finally lost it. Who knew if any of this was real? Who knew if . . .

Then he began to remember. He remembered Jimmy screaming as he gutted him in his shower, his intestines spooling out like a garden hose. He remembered Laura looking up at him with childlike surprise as blood soaked her clothes and her skin turned to chalk. He remembered Bernard moaning, his face in tatters, as Sam spun his head around till his chin rested on his back. He remembered splitting Evan in half like a piece of firewood, shearing Paul's head from his shoulders, and being elbow deep in Dale, his viscera every color of the rainbow, spattered in a prismatic arc that violently clashed with the subdued autumn earth tones of the surrounding woods.

And he remembered coming there. He remembered opening his eyes and seeing the body of the ten-year-old boy, Izzy, white as milk, his throat cleaved nearly to the spine, his blood dripping from the knife in one of Arundel's massive hands, his blood coating the basin that it had recently filled, his blood warming the chalices into which the basin had drained, his blood staining the lips of the witches who raised their chalices to Sam, slick like a newborn, dragged from Hell to serve them.

Sam was on his knees, his face in his hands, screaming and sobbing and pounding his forehead against the cold stone slab. "God," he said . . .

And then he remembered. The most beautiful creature he'd ever seen, who'd opened his eyes and filled him with such hope and purpose. Tall, and golden, and proud, with wings of stardust, saluting them all with his great flaming sword and the crest of the serpent. And Sam in the crowd, his eyes wet with love, raising his own sword and his own serpent crest, in salute to Lucifer.

Sam ground his forehead against the stone slab, the fight gone from him. "Please . . ." he begged.

But he remembered. He remembered the shout that was all words at once blasting them from the celestial city like motes of dust. He remembered screaming and reaching out toward the heavenly light as it grew smaller and vanished, and he remembered plummeting into the endless, swallowing dark.

The chants grew louder, and the stone at Sam's feet turned to mist. The mist began to swirl and sink, trapping his feet and dragging him down. As Sam fought to hang on to this world, his great claws found the familiar grooves he'd worn down deep into this stone slab over the centuries and screeched down them as he was pulled into the vortex.

"We return you now, to your master in Hell," the headmaster said.

Through the swirling mist, Sam could see the fires of Hell. He began to fall. . . .

36

EMBEDDED

Harriet had followed the faithful through the winding tunnels and emerged near the dock. She'd remained at the rear, mummering along with them as the sea grew rough and smashed Sam's boat against the rocks. She'd followed as they'd carried Sam into the Devil's Vale and placed him on a stone altar. She'd watched Headmaster Arundel approach the altar and speak to Sam.

They were going to kill him, this guy who had saved her life. That much seemed clear.

Then again, he was pretty badass. She'd seen that. Maybe if she gave him a fighting chance.

She softly swept together a pile of leaves with her foot. She picked up a leaf and held it over her candle. When it caught, she dropped it into the pile. As it began to smolder, she edged toward the altar.

She fingered the loose brick she'd pocketed in the tunnels. The fire would cause a diversion. She would bash the headmaster over the head with the brick. She would help Sam flee and . . .

. . . and then Sam started to change.

The brick slipped through her fingers and thudded at the headmaster's feet. He turned and saw her. He grabbed her and yanked back her hood.

"Harriet? You know the Devil's Vale is off-limits to students."

He pulled Harriet close. He put a massive hand on her forehead and tilted it back, exposing her throat.

She flailed at his arms and robe. Her hand slipped into his pocket and closed around something soft. A book.

He drew a knife.

And Harriet seized.

She lurched forward so violently, she threw the headmaster judo-style. He sailed through several of the candles on the altar and into the monster.

The chanting stopped. The vortex swirling at the monster's feet collapsed. The monster plunged its fingers into the headmaster's chest and yanked out a good portion of his rib cage. Then it bounded from the altar and descended on the coven.

Harriet jerked helplessly on the ground, staring up at the

starry sky. A head with its jaw missing arced between her and Cassiopeia. An arm spiraled between her and Aquarius. A leg between her and Lacerta.

She'd never realized how many types of screams there were. Low and wet. High-pitched and staccato. Strangled and raspy.

And then the screaming stopped. She thought for a moment the sun was coming up, but then she smelled smoke. Fire was all around her.

Then she was flying. Then she was falling. She hit the dock and lay there, listening to the waves. In the distance, she heard the crackle of trees and saw smoke curl into the night sky.

She felt a breeze. The monster looked down at her, its wings flapping slowly. It reached toward her throat and snapped off her necklace.

Harriet heard a plunk as the necklace hit the water. Then she felt the dock shudder as the monster took to the skies.

37

REUNION

S o. You okay?" her dad asked for the fifteenth time today, trying to sound casual.

"I'm fine, Dad. Thanks for . . . baby-proofing my room."

"That's not what it is," her dad said, testing one of the heavy rubber bumpers he'd put on everything vaguely resembling a corner.

"Might be simpler to just swathe me in Bubble Wrap."

"We're just doing . . . you know . . . safety . . ." he said, quietly taking all her pencils. "So. You okay?"

She had just returned from the Caanan Falls Wellness Center. What had triggered Harriet's breakdown remained a mystery. All anyone knew for certain was that a fire had started on the south side of Danforth Putnam. Scoopers were dispatched from the mainland to control the blaze, but not before it claimed all of what was called the Devil's Vale and much of the woods north of it.

The coast guard managed, thankfully, to evacuate all the students, but not without considerable confusion, as much of the faculty appeared to be missing. Charred remains were found in the vale after the fire was put out, and it was believed that these might have belonged to the teachers, but they were so far gone it was hard to tell. As to why they had all gathered in the vale, no one could say. Except for Harriet, who seemed to have suffered some sort of psychotic break. She offered a rambling tale about witches and demons, culminating in hysterical screaming and catatonia. Her parents raised bloody hell when they found out the cops had questioned her without their permission, contributing to the growing pile of litigations and investigations swirling about Danforth Putnam, which was now closed indefinitely.

When she'd first arrived at the Caanan Falls Wellness Center, Harriet wouldn't speak. She would scream, usually when snapping awake from a nightmare, but didn't form words for weeks. When she finally began talking, she had no memory of anything leading up to the fire. Doctors considered using hypnosis to retrieve her memories, but her neurologist adamantly opposed this for fear it might induce a seizure. Despite the memory loss, she improved steadily, and Dr. Spellman believed she could now return home under supervised care.

"You ready for some lunch, sweetie?" Her mom entered with a grilled cheese and soup. She was smiling. She was always smiling these days. At least with her mouth. Her eyes . . . Harriet couldn't remember the last time she'd seen her mother blink.

"Thanks, Mom. You guys can leave me alone for a minute. I just want to unpack. If that's okay."

"Of course!" Her mother almost screamed in an effort to sound cheerful. "We'll be right outside if you need us." She grinned and backed out of the room with Harriet's dad, tugging the door shut. Harriet heard her mom sniffle as she walked away, heard her dad whisper something he probably meant to be encouraging but which, from the sound of it, only made her mom angry.

Harriet looked at the boxes of her things from Danforth Putnam. They were taped tightly shut, and she would have to open them without the aid of anything remotely sharp.

She was making real progress with the edge of a meditation cassette when she felt a breeze. She turned toward her closed window.

Sam was sitting in a chair staring at her. He looked human, except for the shadow on the wall behind him, which had horns, a long snaking tail and giant, flapping wings.

"Long time," Sam said.

Harriet dropped the cassette.

"Remember me?"

She nodded.

"Remember what happened?"

She nodded again. Tears rolled down her cheeks.

A cigarette appeared between his fingers. He waved it, and it was lit. He took a puff, then looked around nervously.

"Oh, shoot. I don't want your parents to think you're . . ."

He tapped the window, which shot open. A breeze carried the smoke outside. He rubbed his fingers and the cigarette vanished.

Harriet swallowed. "Are you going to kill me?"

He raised his eyebrows. "Wasn't planning on it."

She tried to catch her breath. "What are you?"

Sam stiffened and crossed his arms. He looked offended. "What are *you*?" he asked.

"Am I crazy?" she whispered.

Sam shrugged. "One thing I'm not is a shrink."

"Why are you here?"

Sam rose from the chair and ambled around the room.

"Just wanted to make sure you were okay. We're friends and . . . no one fucks with my friends."

Harriet stared at him in shock. "We're friends?"

"Well, you did free me. Where I come from, debts are taken pretty seriously. Consider me your guardian . . . something."

He drew a finger across the top of the box she was working on and it sprang open.

"Don't you have a scissors or something?"

"My parents are worried . . . Once, at the center, I tried to hurt myself."

"No kidding?" Sam said jovially. "Me too. After the picnic you crashed, I tried to end it in a bunch of different ways. Turns out I can't. How much does that suck?"

He gently split open the remaining boxes.

"I am stuck here. I think. If I've learned anything, it's that I don't know much. In fact, the only thing I can tell you with any certainty is what I want. So. Where's that book?"

Harriet took a few breaths, then hoisted the suitcase she'd brought home from the center onto her bed. She unlatched it, fished around beneath some clothes and found a small leather book.

She'd been gripping it so hard when they found her at the dock that they couldn't pry it from her hands until she was sedated, so it went with her to the center, along with what she'd been wearing. When she could finally talk, she told them it was for D&D. That's all it took for them to lose interest in it.

"I looked at it every day."

"Why?" Sam asked.

"To prove I wasn't crazy."

"I can't let you keep it."

"How come?" Harriet asked.

"If I did, they might come for you."

"Who?"

Sam rubbed his face. "Danforth Putnam was founded in 1654. That book is from the eleventh century. What does that tell you?"

Didn't end with him. That's what Flynn had told Harriet about Alderhut and the witchcraft at Danforth Putnam. Maybe it didn't start with him either.

"You think there's more of them?"

"I thought I might look into it. It's not like I'm pressed for time." Sam leafed through the book. The wings in Sam's shadow flexed. The tail lashed angrily. "I want to know who wrote this. I want to know how they learned this. I want to know if there are other books like this. I want to know how deep and wide it all goes."

"What are you going to do if you find any of them?"

Sam smiled at her. "Guess."

Harriet tried to swallow but found she could not. She mopped her eyes with her sleeve. Despite the open window, the room had become incredibly warm.

Sam looked at her, his eyes gentle and sad. "I'd take your memories away, if I could." He looked back at the book and grunted. "I'd take mine away, if I could."

"You could take mine away," she whispered.

He looked up. "What?"

"You could take my memories away." She was staring at him, terrified, but pleading. "You could take everything away."

He stared back at her for a long while. "I won't do that,"

he said softly. Tears spilled down her face. He held her gaze. "*You* won't do that," he said. "I won't let you."

She sniffled. "I need some Kleenex."

He hunted down a box and handed it to her. "But, you know, if anyone fucks with you . . ."

Her eyes widened, and she shook her head frantically. "No. No."

He smiled. "I won't get carried away. I got my shit . . . more or less under control." He frowned, puzzled. "I think."

"Honey?"

Harriet's mom was knocking while entering. Harriet gasped and looked at Sam. He was gone.

"How was the grilled cheese?" her mother brayed with a painful smile. "I used the Gruyère I got from the . . . Oh." She noticed the uneaten lunch. "Didn't you like it?"

"I just got distracted unpacking," Harriet said.

"Sweetie, have you been crying?"

Harriet dissolved into tears again. Her mother raced across the room and held her. "It's going to be all right, baby. It's going to be all right."

Harriet squeezed her eyes shut. Through the window Sam had opened, she heard a pigeon flapping, a squirrel chittering, a neighbor's lawn mower, the tang of a four-square ball getting spiked, the whir of bike gears shifting and the whoop of a preteen gang on ten-speeds, the creak of a pram and the cry of a baby. She desperately tried to grab all those sounds and erase herself within them, dissolve into their placid suburban normalcy. But she could not. They all seemed too fragile, vaporous, fake.

"I feel . . ." Harriet said, quaking, "so . . . alone."

"You're not, sweetie," her mother said, rocking her like a baby, her own tears coursing into her daughter's hair. "You're not. You're not. You're not."

And that was true, Harriet realized. The terrifying orphic forces she had prodded would never leave her alone again. She had gazed into the abyss, and now the abyss was gazing back.

Nietzsche had said something like that. Harriet's English teacher, Mr. Lutz, used to blather on about Nietzsche. Nietzsche admired the Greeks, Mr. Lutz said, because they'd had the courage to laugh at the absurdity of their own existence. Nietzsche hugged a horse one day and went crazy, and Mr. Lutz was now probably just some of the moldering bones collected from the vale, tagged, brushed and arranged on a tarp in a police lab somewhere.

Harriet started shaking in her mother's arms. "Oh, sweetie, it's okay. We're going to get you back to normal. It's just . . . are you . . . are you laughing?"

Harriet looked up at her mom and nodded. "Normal." She dissolved into giggles. Harriet had never been normal. And she took some spiteful joy in the realization that normal had been an illusion all along.

Her mother watched, alarmed, as Harriet walked to the

window and stared out at their manicured neighborhood. Everything she had ever worried about, none of it mattered. It was all just brume and noise. She felt dizzy. But giddy. Vertiginous. Untethered. Wild. And terrifyingly, terrifyingly—

"Sweetie," her mom whispered, "what's going on? What . . . how are you feeling?"

Harriet turned to her mother, grinning, her face shining with tears. "Free."

Acknowledgments

I'd like to thank my wife, Carrie, for always being my first and best reader. No one is more supportive of her fellow writers. I'd like to thank my managers, Jonathan Berry and Oly Obst, for not laughing when I said I had a novella I wanted to sell, and for putting it in the hands of Richard Abate, who managed, miraculously, to sell it. For my editor, Mark Tavani, there is no thanks great enough. He took a long short story and worked with me patiently and tirelessly to turn it into a novel. I feel bad for anyone who has to write a book without him. I'd like to thank Danielle Dieterich, who thought of the title for this book, and I'd like to thank everyone else at Putnam who worked so diligently on it. I'd like to thank all my friends and family who read early versions of this story and shared invaluable feedback. And I'd like to thank my daughters, Delainy and Adeline, who inspire everything I do.